Serving HIM

An Alpha Billionaire Romance

Vol. II

By

M.S. Parker

And

Cassie Wild

Table of Contents

Chapter 1 1

Chapter 2 7

Chapter 3 21

Chapter 4 33

Chapter 5 49

Chapter 6 55

Chapter 7 65

Chapter 8 75

Chapter 9 85

Chapter 10 93

Chapter 11 101

Acknowledgement 121

About The Authors 122

- MS Parker 122
- Cassie Wild 122

Chapter 1

Aleena

"Good morning."

I nearly crashed into Dominic Monday morning. It was six-fifteen and I'd been awake since a little before five, barely able to sleep.

I hadn't seen him since our oddly tense lunch on Saturday and, although I was certain I'd been imagining it, I could have sworn his eyes slid over me when I wasn't watching, that they'd linger on my mouth, my breasts...lower.

When I all but toppled over in my attempt to stop our collision, his hands came up and caught my arms, steadying me. My heart gave an odd, hiccupping sort of beat as his hands fell away, without even a hint of a pause.

"Good morning, Mr. Snow," I said, stepping

back at the exact moment he did.

"Are you ready to get to work?" he asked, giving me a polite, distant smile.

It took me until we got back into the main room to realize that he was talking to me differently. There was no warmth in his voice, not like before. He wasn't being cold, exactly, but it was definitely all business. Not even a hint of flirting.

I should've been grateful. The last thing I needed was a boss who felt like he could openly flirt with his employees. I didn't want that. Still, I couldn't help but feel a pang when I thought about how much I'd enjoyed his light, subtle flirtations up until now.

"We've already talked about how you're welcome to use the kitchen," he said as we headed down the steps to the first floor. "But Francisco is coming in today. If there's anything you'd like to have ordered in, let him know."

He paused and lifted a brow. "Be warned...you don't want to use anything of his without letting him know. He's temperamental."

Francisco. Mentally, I compared that name to the list I'd spent the weekend committing to memory. He was the chef who came in a few days a week. He spent the rest of the week at the main house—which, I now knew, was another property of Dominic's.

Other staff here at the penthouse included Dominic's household manager. She wasn't exactly a butler, as Dominic didn't like to have a lot of people invade his personal space here, but she managed the cleaning personnel and helped arranged any events that might take place at the penthouse.

There was also a chef at the house in the Hamptons, a groundskeeper who headed an entire crew of landscapers, a butler at the main house, a household manager at the main house, a crew of housekeepers...the list went on and on.

Each of the people in charge were responsible for hiring's and firing's, but they might occasionally reach out to the household manager, or if she wasn't available, to me. That wasn't likely to happen any time soon, but she wanted me to be prepared and she'd be introducing me over the coming weeks so I'd be familiar with all of them.

"Whatever you want to have on hand for breakfast, make sure you note it down. Lauren or Cisco will make sure it's here, okay?" he said as he opened the refrigerator and took out an energy drink. "You need to feel comfortable here."

I nodded.

"Obviously, here in the city, there will be more interaction between us since there isn't a separate entrance. Feel free to entertain around work, but I do ask that, unless we've talked about it, you limit it to your quarters. I don't usually have parties here, but I do bring home women from time to time and it could be awkward if we both had company in the same place."

I tried not to think about my own fantasies of being one of those women he brought home. Or the pang I felt when I thought about him having sex with someone else.

"Since you have the guest house in the Hamptons, I don't really care what you do there, as long as it doesn't interfere with your work."

I nodded again, acting like I was filing all of this away even though I was actually still trying to process everything that was happening. What he was talking about right now didn't really matter anyway. I had one friend in the city and no romantic interest in anyone—unless of course I considered my bathroom fantasies. I wasn't planning on bringing anyone back here or to the Hamptons anytime soon.

The sound of the door opening was followed by a quick and cheerful, "Hello!"

A grin flashed over Dominic's face, one that brought a rush of heat to my belly and a knot to my throat. I wanted to see him smile like that when I greeted him.

And how silly was that?

Fawna appeared in the doorway and looked between us. "Well, the two of you are already up and moving."

"You know me," Dominic said, tipping his drink in her direction.

"Yes, I do." She gave him a smile and then turned her friendly eyes toward me. "And Aleena...did you get settled in?"

"Yes." Some of my tension faded away. "Mostly. I've gone over the paperwork you've given me, too."

"Please tell me you didn't spend your entire weekend working." She *tsked* under her breath.

"No." I glanced at Dominic and then back at Fawna. "I was able to get some shopping done as well. I needed to expand my wardrobe."

"Ahhh...yes. That was actually going to be on the schedule for today."

"I..." I blinked. "What?"

Dominic folded his arms. "Your wardrobe. I told Fawna I wanted her to take you shopping."

"I've been shopping," I said. I gestured at the neat black suit I wore. I knew they couldn't find fault with it. It was Chanel. It cost two hundred dollars...*used*. There wasn't anything wrong with it.

Dominic opened his mouth, but Fawna held up a hand and stepped between us. "I see you have. That's a lovely suit, Aleena. It's very flattering."

I angled my chin up, fighting the urge to glare at the man standing behind Fawna.

"You'll need more than one or two nice pieces for the job as my assistant, Aleena," Dominic said, his voice flat.

"I can buy my own clothing," I retorted.

Something that might have been surprise flashed through his eyes.

Fawna, ever the peacemaker, cut in again. "Aleena, perhaps you'll allow me to look at your wardrobe. I have a good idea what you'll need—I'm

5

sure you can agree there."

"I..." I stopped and then nodded.

"Wonderful. And if you are amenable, then you'll allow Dominic to help you with your...wardrobe expansions." She winked at me. "After all, you understand that your appearance reflects on Dominic and the Winter Corporation, yes?"

I fought the urge to grit my teeth as I mentally counted to ten, then back. Finally, I looked from her to Dominic. "I don't believe in letting somebody pay my way," I said quietly. Then I looked away. "But fine. I'll let you buy a *few* pieces. Enough to last me a few weeks. After that, I'll start buying a piece a week with *my own money.*"

"Aleena, it's not like I can't afford—"

"Perfectly reasonable," Fawna said, interrupting Dominic.

Chapter 2

Aleena

I was *exhausted.*

The past week had been a whirlwind of work, shopping, work, studying, work, and more work.

I don't think I spent so much time cramming since college.

I'd committed a ridiculous amount of material to memory—it wasn't something I talked about, and I didn't like to, either. At school, I had noted how people reacted when they figured out my talent—they didn't like it. But my memory was phenomenal. I'd never had to note orders down at any of the restaurants where I worked. I just repeated them back once and I had them nailed.

Something a little more complicated required me to write it down, but once I did, it was stored in my memory. So my work-around was to take Fawna's notes and write them down, organizing them in a way that worked better for me.

Now I just hoped it came in handy.

Fawna wasn't here.

She was spending the weekend at the hospital with her little grandson and...oh, my, goodness. What a *cutie*. When I'd asked about him, she told me that she'd love to take me up to see him so that was how I'd spent my Friday night, visiting with her and tiny little Eli.

He was so small. I'd seen dolls bigger than him. His wizened little face had stared up at us with somber eyes.

Pushing aside the thoughts of Eli and Fawna, I focused on the house that had just come into view. I almost had to pick my jaw up on the floor and I amended the term. That wasn't a house.

Mansion, I guess.

It was massive. Five families could have easily fit in there and I had no idea how many acres of land the house sat on. The attached garage could probably house ten or twelve cars.

The car came to a halt in front of a smaller house. Smaller compared to the other house, at least.

"Maxwell?" I asked quietly.

The driver of the car glanced into his mirror as he put the car into park. "Yes, Ms. Davison?"

"Is this..." I paused and cleared my throat. "Would this be the guest house?"

"It would." He smiled.

I didn't let myself gape.

Okay, I'd known Dominic was rich, but suddenly, *rich* was taking on a whole different meaning.

I opened the door and received a censuring gaze from the driver. "I can open the door, Max," I said.

"So can I and I'm paid to do it," he countered.

"But I feel silly letting somebody open a door I'm perfectly capable of opening myself." He looked as though he wanted to argue, but then he finally just sighed and shook his head, a faintly exasperated but amused smile on his face.

As Maxwell took my bags out of the trunk, I automatically reached for one. He gave me one of those stern looks that some older gentlemen can give without being condescending. According to the files Fawna had given me, Maxwell had been driving for the Snow family since he was nineteen and had followed Dominic when he'd moved out. I'd seen Maxwell with Dominic and it was clear there was a tight bond between them.

"Do you want these in the master bedroom, Ms. Davison?" he asked as he followed me to the door. This time, I noticed what I hadn't before. Maxwell was British.

"Ah...call me Aleena, please?" I gave him my best smile as I thought it through. I hadn't realized there was more than one bedroom. "Use the master bedroom, please." Why not, I figured. I was the only one staying here, right?

"Of course." He disappeared down the hall to

the right and I made a mental note. When he returned, he asked, "Will there be anything else you need from me? Mr. Snow said to let you know there are some nice shops nearby if you'd like to go shopping."

Shopping...I made a face and although I could have been imagining it, I thought I saw Maxwell hide a smile. "I'm tired of shopping, Max." I paused and then asked, "Do you mind if I call you Max?"

"No." A faint smile crossed his lips. "My wife used to call me Max."

"You're married?"

Now the smile on his lips took on a sad slant. "I was, yes. She died a few years ago."

"I'm sorry."

"Thank you."

Looking away, I brushed my hair back. "I think I'll get familiar with the property, meet the staff inside the house before I worry about the shops in town."

After Maxwell had left, I wandered the guesthouse.

It was nearly as big as the entire penthouse. I had never imagined I'd fall into anything like this. It wasn't *mine* and I knew this. It was mine for now, though. And I still couldn't figure out how I'd lucked into this. That was what it felt like—I'd lucked into this.

The guesthouse had a living room with a deluxe flat screen TV and long, low sofas that were more comfortable than anything I'd ever known.

There was a separate dining area that was far too formal. One look into the kitchen told me that I'd be spending most of my time eating in there. The kitchen made me want to jump around and clap my hands. And somebody had stocked it. I couldn't help but smile when I peeked into cabinets and the fridge. I had a feeling whoever the somebody was had a direct line straight to Fawna. Somehow, the things I tended to eat were already on hand,

My exploration revealed a linen closet, a laundry room and then a spare bedroom—it was lavish and luxurious, but I knew it was the spare bedroom because it was down the left hallway.

If I hadn't known better, I would have thought it was the master bedroom. With the dove gray walls and rich maroon accents, it was almost too beautiful to be real.

But then I found the master bedroom.

It looked like springtime.

Pale green walls, the carpet a sea of blue. Both colors twined in the bed set. When I stroked my hand down it, I was almost certain that it was real silk. Upon closer inspection, I saw that walls weren't simply green, but hand-painted.

Tiny little swirls of green on green.

The king-sized bed looked like living trees rising up out of the carpet, spiraling up, the branches as perfect as if they truly were tree trunks.

Oh, yeah.

11

I was sleeping in the master bedroom. If I had my way, I'd never *leave* here.

Moving deeper into the bedroom, I found myself touching everything. There was no obvious place to store my clothing so I went to open one of the paneled doors and when it swung open, I stepped back, gasping in surprise at the TV there. It was almost as big as the TV out in the living room and one of those curved screens I'd seen advertised recently.

Wow.

I didn't think anything could top that bedroom, but then I slid open the final set of louvered doors and this time, I couldn't stop myself from gaping.

The bathroom was indescribable. Pillars surrounded the sunken Jacuzzi tub. On the far side of the bathroom, there were as a glass-in shower big enough for a party of five.

The toilet was enclosed and set apart from the rest of the room and to my delight, there was a padded vanity with a lighted mirror.

I felt like a frickin' princess.

Maybe the castle wasn't mine, but I still felt like a princess.

***

I had keys to the main house.

With those clutched in my hand, I made my way up to what I was now calling the *real* castle—at least in my head.

But I didn't have a chance to use them. I'd

followed the path that led from my guesthouse up to the main house and by the time I got there, the door opened.

"You must be Aleena!"

I found myself face to face with a beaming woman who would have been about my mother's age, if she hadn't died when I was so young.

"Ah...hi." I smiled at her, and recalled a name from the list of employees. "Janice?"

I don't know how it was possible, but the smile on her face widened. "That would be me." She swung a coat around her shoulders as she stepped aside. "I'm on my way into town—a bit of shopping to get done. Is there anything I can get for you?"

"No." I managed a smile. "I'm good. I noticed that someone had stocked the kitchen at the guesthouse...was that you?"

"It was. Did I miss anything?"

"No." I shook my head and glanced around the kitchen. "I was going to take a look around. Should I wait?"

"Of course not." She patted at her pockets. "Use those keys. I'll be back in a few hours, as will the others. You can meet them all then, but you can take a look around, familiarize yourself with everything. Mr. Snow is in his quarters. He's got a guest with him." She hesitated and then added, "Just so you know."

"Okay." There was something in her voice, something in the way she watched me. I gave her a nod, uncertain what she was trying to relay.

She seemed satisfied with my response, though and turned. "I assume Fawna provided you with all my information, just in case?"

"Yes." I had an entire category now, on my phone—a new one, courtesy of Dominic—that was full of nothing but contacts for Dominic's Hampton House. Another that was for The Main House, and another for The Penthouse. One that was The Winter Corporation, one for Family and one for Friends...all in all, I had hundreds of contacts programed into my phone and only five of them were friends of *mine*.

A few minutes later, she was out the door and I was left alone. The first thing I did was pull up the map of the Hampton house that Fawna had provided me with.

I scanned it, oriented myself and gave strict mental instructions to stay away from the section I knew to be Dominic's quarters. His *quarters*, so to speak, took up most of the west wing.

That left the east wing and the main part of the house for me to explore.

It took me nearly half an hour just to cover the first floor. There was a small indoor pool and I peeked into the garage and saw that I'd been right— there were seven cars inside and it could easily hold five more. The sun was starting to set, throwing shadows across the stairs as I walked up them.

I finished my self-guided tour. I cast the west

wing another curious glance, but I had absolutely no desire to go anywhere if I might run into Dominic and a *guest*. That guest was female.

Dominic had made it clear he wanted his privacy and I'd give him that.

I'd also save myself the jealousy—

Yeah, girl. You're really doing that, I thought sourly as a twinge of it dug its way into my heart and twisted deep.

Something cracked.

I jerked to a stop at the sound and whipped my head around.

It came again, followed by a low, rough noise.

What was—?

It came again and I found myself following the noise. I don't know if it was foolishness or concern. Then I heard it again.

In high school—those hated, hated years—I'd found myself ostracized even more when I came across the football captain in the middle of a fight with his girlfriend. He'd backhanded her, slapping her across the face and the sound was one I'd never forget.

That sound was a lot like the one echoing through the halls now.

Maybe it was fury that drove me, just as it had then. I'd lunged between them and swung my Calculus textbook at the big, arrogant jock, catching him off-guard. When he'd gone to hit me, I'd swung again and then kicked him in the knee, the way my dad had taught me.

He'd gone down and when he fell, he broke his arm. Goodbye, regional championships.

I found myself reliving that moment as I raced around the corner and there, I froze. Because now I could hear the other sound. A moan. A low, rough moan and it brought a rush of heat to my cheeks.

Turn around, I told myself. *You said you'd respect his privacy.*

I almost did stop.

But I heard that harsh, heavy sound again, followed by another long, deep moan.

I had to look.

If there was somebody being hurt, I'd never be able to live with myself.

Carefully, I edged down the hallway, reaching into my pocket to pull out my cellphone. Automatically, I silenced the ringer. I peered inside the door. It was mostly shut, but not enough.

Day-yum.

Dominic was naked. Golden tanned skin covered every glorious inch of him, muscles rippling as he moved. Broad shoulders tapered down to a narrow waist and from my angle, I had the perfect view of his perfect ass.

Seriously, it was like a work of art, firm and muscled and round.

I stood there, my mouth hanging open, he shifted position slightly and I watched as he brought one hand up, wrapped it around his cock and gave it a slow, thorough stroking.

He shifted again and my gaze landed on his back.

Eyes widening, I saw something I hadn't seen before. Granted, I'd been a little preoccupied and a lot thrown off-balance, but he had scars. Scars the like I had never seen before. Not that I have a lot of experience, but my brain didn't know how to process what I was looking at.

Thwack.

I jumped at the sound and shifted my gaze.

He wasn't alone and he wasn't the one moaning.

There was a naked woman in there with him...and she was tied up, her arms bound overhead to the bedpost. To the rings—oh my god, my mind flashed back to the bed back at the penthouse. To the rings. Fuck. Dominic—he was—okay, he was...

Shit.

Her arms were stretched high, her wrists tied with strips of cloth, attached to the tall wooden bedpost at the base of the bed, facing away from me. And as I watched, Dominic brought his hand down on her ass again. Which would explain why it was a startling shade of pink.

She made a low, husky noise.

I had to bite my lower lip to keep from doing the same. A hard, heavy throb echoed down deep inside and, to my horror, my clit began to pulse. He spanked her again, and my clit pulsed as though I was the one standing there, and not over here, an uninvited guest to their little party.

I pressed my hand against my chest, surprised to feel how hard my heart was beating against my ribs. *Leave,* I told myself as Dominic bent over and grabbed something. A moment later, I saw that it was a condom.

He was getting ready to...oh. No. I needed to leave. I can't watch them...

You're already watching it, a gleeful little voice thought. *If you can watch it, have the guts to think it. You're watching them fuck.*

I watched, mesmerized, as Dominic rolled a condom over his cock. I knew I shouldn't have stayed, but I couldn't look away.

It wasn't just Dominic, though. It was the sheer, unadulterated hunger and the way everything about her seemed to *beg* for more. For his touch, for his body, for the hard blow of his hand on her ass.

Spanking was something I'd always associated with children and punishment. A firm crack on the behind for something done wrong. Absolutely nothing sexual or sensual about it. I'd never understood the people who'd used it that way.

Now, though...

"Do you want me to stop?" Dominic's voice was low, but not out of control. "You know what you have to say."

I swallowed hard.

"Speak, Maya, or I'm going to get my belt and you won't be able to sit for a week."

I shivered, and reflexively, I found myself clenching my buttocks, just as this unknown woman, Maya, was. Need twisted low inside me.

"Fuck me." On the other side of the door, Maya gasped. "Damn it! Fuck me!"

"That's not what I want. Say what I want to hear." Dominic wrapped her ponytail around his hand and yanked her head back. "This is the last time I'm going to ask."

I wasn't sure which I wanted more: to see what would happen if she didn't say it, or see what happened if she did.

"Please, sir."

My nails dug into my palm and the wetness between my thighs gathered. I'd never be able to look at him and call him *sir* without remember this again. *Never.*

"Please, fuck me."

The last word turned into a wail as Dominic slammed into her with one thrust. I bit my bottom lip, wondering what it must feel like, being empty one moment and full the next. I wondered if it hurt. He was so big. The one guy I'd had sex with hadn't even been close to that size, and it had hurt. But Maya didn't sound like she was in pain.

In fact, as she threw back of her head and screamed, I was pretty damn certain she was enjoying herself. And it made me look back on the one pitiful sexual encounter I'd had with even more dismay.

Okay, so I'd been a kid and it hadn't been much fun, but now I *really* felt cheated.

Chapter 3

Dominic

Trouver L'Amour would open to clients on Valentine's Day with a lavish masquerade ball.

Planning it with Fawna over the past few months had been more fun—and more intense and stressful—than I could imagine. You want to have a Valentine bash in New York City? Start planning it a few years in advance. Also, stock up on aspirin and alcohol.

Fawna was still nonplussed when it came to my...less than mainstream sex life, but we had a similar view when it came to anything resembling a romantic relationship. They were fine for other people, but not for us. We didn't need a significant other to make ourselves feel better or special. We didn't have the time or the patience for building trust and pretending to care about what other people thought or felt. We certainly had no time for mending the hurt feelings that would inevitably come with any sort of romantic relationship.

Our only real relationship was with each other. There were a few other casual friends, but the truth was, I was closer to my personal assistant than anybody else in life.

Now how fucked up is that?

We knew each other's thoughts and moods. There was no pretense between us. When you see people at their worst, it had the tendency to either completely destroy a friendship or solidify it.

Fawna and I had seen each other at our worst—and I loved her as much as I was capable of loving somebody. There was nothing romantic to it. She was, plain and simply put, my closest friend in the world.

And she was leaving.

I understood. There was no doubt about that, but I'd miss her.

After this party, she was going to quietly withdraw. The two of us had both been surprised with how easily Aleena had taken to the job Fawna had turned over to her.

The slow burning attraction I felt for my new PA was still there—and it was no longer quite so slow burning, but it wasn't happening. Down that way lay trouble—and possibly lawsuits.

The past three weeks hadn't come and gone without pitfalls—especially the first few days after the trip to the Hamptons. Aleena had been stiff and awkward, hardly looking at me with direct eye contact and I wondered if, perhaps, Maya had said something to her, but once we got back to the city, she'd slowly relaxed.

She had more steel to her than I'd expected. It drove me crazy even as it drew me to her.

I was still aggravated about the shopping thing.

I'd dragged it out of Fawna. She'd gone shopping at consignment stores—*consignment* stores. I'd given her a damned credit card and she could have gone *anywhere*, but she'd preferred to stick with the clothing she'd already picked up. Fawna had talked her into buying a few more pieces, but it had been very few.

The only high-end purchases had been Fawna's doing, several cocktail gowns that Fawna had rightly insisted Aleena would need.

Now, caught up in a debate with Aleena, Fawna and one Mrs. Irene Dudeck—the party planner Fawna had insisted we hire—I tried not to let myself get distracted by Aleena.

It was hard—no, almost impossible.

The one blessing in disguise was the one I hadn't wanted, Irene Dudeck.

Irene was good at what she did, but she was also on the hunt for husband number three. I didn't mind that nearly fifteen years separated us. I minded that she watched me with avid dollar signs in her eyes.

But just then, she was focused on the party and the dollars it would bring. Her overly high laugh kept interrupting my daydreams. Daydreams that had to do with me seeing Aleena stretched out over my bed, her warm skin gleaming soft against my sheets, then blushing to rose after I brought my hand down on that ripe, firm ass.

"Candlelight," Aleena suggested. "Candlelight, a few roses at the table and some mirrors. Keep it subtle, keep it simple. If this is a masquerade ball, people are going to want to keep the focus on them anyway—*and* you want them thinking about *Trouver L'Amour*."

Candlelight...I could get behind that idea.

"Nonsense," Irene said, sniffing. "That's clichéd. We want something with a little more mystery. Silk wall hangings." She tapped her lips and her face lit up with a smile. "Champagne silk! I know just the thing!"

"No." I straightened up and shot Irene a look. "We're running out of time. I think simple is the best idea."

"Why..." Irene drew herself up and stared at me. "Mr. Snow, I *assure* you that I can handle this. My staff and I—"

"Are very good at what you do, but you won't be able to see the vision I have inside my head. I want simple elegance." I gave her a smile and reached out, brushing my fingers across the back of her hand. "You have to admit, Irene. Nothing beats the flicker of candlelight across a woman's skin for sheer elegance. As for mystery...a woman, in and of

24

herself, is all the mystery we'll need."

As Irene smiled and leaned my way, I saw Aleena share a quick glance with Fawna. Their expressions were poised and perfectly professional. Yet, I had the feeling they were both smirking at me.

A short while later, after I'd escorted a flustered Irene to the door, I turned and glared at Fawna.

"Problem?"

Fawna had been with me too long to be thrown by the curt tone.

"Not at all." She gave me a serene smile and asked, "Would you like me to send a personal invitation for Ms. Dudeck? I'm sure she'd love to...mystify you personally at the ball, Dominic."

I snarled at her and then shifted my glare to Aleena. When all she did was give me an inquiring smile, I jabbed a finger at her. I was pissed off and being an asshole and I didn't care. I was fed up with the frustration of wanting her. Fed up with there being nothing I could do about it. I could only imagine kissing that unseen smirk off her face and leaving her panting and aching—as desperate for me as I was becoming for her.

No. No...I don't do this.

"You'll have to do better than that, Ms. Davison," I said, biting each word off. "If you can't sit with an event planner and act more professionally than that, then this isn't going to work out."

Her lashes fluttered.

25

I braced myself, waiting for the snap of her temper—I'd come to appreciate it, even found it amusing, and sometimes, a welcome change.

But what I saw was a flash of shock. Her nostrils flared slightly and a flush of color appeared on her cheeks.

"I apologize, Mr. Snow."

Her phone rang. "Turn that damn thing off," I barked.

"Dominic!" Fawna snapped at me.

"I'm tired of that damn thing ringing when I'm trying to have a conversation."

Aleena backed away. "I'll take care of the call, if that's acceptable, sir."

She inclined her head and turned, walking quickly away. As the door closed behind her, Fawna rounded on me. "What is the matter with you?"

"I..." Snapping my jaw shut, I realized I had no answer.

The door opened and Aleena stood there. "Mr. Snow, it's your mother. Are you available?"

Well, *fuck.*

I held out a hand, looking at Aleena's face, but she had her head slightly bowed, her eyes downcast. "I'll wait out in my office," she said quietly as she turned the phone over.

Helpless, I lifted the phone to my ear. Closing my eyes, I said, "Hi, Mom."

"What's this I hear about a party, darling?"

Skipping the small talk, are we, Mom?

26

"It's not a party, Mom," I said with a sigh. "It's for *Trouver L'Amour*. For clients."

"But they're clients from our social circle, darling. People who know me and respect me."

I wasn't so sure about that last part. *Respect* wasn't really all that big in our inner circle. People respected money, and they respected power. But respecting the person? That wasn't something we saw much of.

More and more, that was bothering me. I found my eyes straying to the closed door between Aleena and me.

"You're welcome to come, Mom." I knew that was only part of what she wanted, but if I gave in to this right away, I was hoping it'd move things along a bit faster. "I just didn't think you'd want to spend your Valentine's Day mingling with people during a match-making soiree."

"And where else would I spend it?"

Now we were getting closer to it. "Aren't you going to spend it with Richard?" I named the latest in a long list of 'companions' my mother had had since the divorce. The last two had gone to school with me at one point or another.

"Richard," she scoffed. "I dumped him ages ago. He was only after my money."

Translation: he found someone just as rich, but younger.

"I'm sorry to hear that, Mom," I said softly.

"Well, water under the bridge, as they say," she

said, her voice taking on a tragic, noble air.

That was my mother. Even as I thought it, guilt stabbed at me. I hadn't had a good relationship with her for...well. Maybe I'd never had one. Even after my life had gone to shit in my teens, things hadn't gone well for us. I hadn't been the sweet little delight she'd hoped for—not that she'd ever told me that to my face, but I knew I'd been more trouble than she'd planned on when she adopted me.

At least she did love me, though.

My dad...? Once it became clear how very scarred and ruined and broken I was, how damaged I'd probably always be, he'd decided then and there to wash his hands of me.

I thought of the woman on the other end of the phone.

Of us.

Clearing my throat, I said softly, "I'd love for you to come to the party, Mom."

Things hadn't always been easy, but she'd been there, even if she hadn't known what to do or what to say after. She'd been there.

Dad had just walked away.

"Thank you," she said, sounding mildly surprised.

"Okay." Feeling awkward now, I looked around my office and immediately wished I hadn't. Fawna stood exactly where she had been and her gaze was sheer fire. "Ah...okay, I need to get back to work. More things to wrap up for the party."

"Very well. I'll see you Saturday. Oh...I heard that Penelope Rittenour will be attending. I'm sure she'd love to have some time with you, Dominic. She so enjoys your company."

I reminded myself that this was neither the time nor the place to go back to that discussion. "All right, Mom. I'll send out an official invitation in today's mail, and I'll see you on Saturday."

"Lovely, darling," she chirped. "Till then."

Dropping Aleena's phone onto my desk, I braced my hands on the surface.

Fawna said nothing.

"Get it out," I said, staring at the neatly stacked and labeled folders. They bore Aleena's handwriting now, not Fawna's. She was taking to this job too easily, too quickly. It would have been better, I decided, if she'd just sucked at it.

"Get what out?" Fawna asked sweetly. "Tell you that you're being an ass? Oh, I don't think I need to mention that, dear. You already know."

I shot her a dark look and then snatched up the phone.

I opened the door, an apology already forming on my tongue. Apologies were like medicine, I'd always tried to tell myself. Best to get them over and done with.

But Aleena was on the phone on her desk, busily writing.

"Yes...yes." She glanced up at me and then away. "I understand. I'll be sure to give him the message,

Ms. Rittenour."

A moment later, she disconnected and then tore off the notepad. It bore the Winter Corporation logo and beneath it was Penelope's name and phone number. She also gave me two more pieces of paper. "You had three calls, Mr. Snow."

"Fuck them," I said, grabbing the notes and wadding them up. "Let's go out to lunch. Want to try Bouley's?"

"I'm already eating." She gestured at a small bar on her desk. "And I'm afraid neither of us will have time for much. One of the numbers you just threw away was Ms. Dudeck's. She called. There's been an emergency with the band. The lead singer woke up this morning with no voice. He has severe laryngitis and will be unable to perform."

The apology I'd been trying to drag back up my throat died as I processed her words.

"You..." I fisted a hand in my hair and tugged. "Please tell me you're saying this just to get back at me for being an asshole."

"Of course not, sir. I'm simply passing on your messages as you hired me to do."

"Aleena!" I wanted to grab her now, grab her and shake.

"Yes, Mr. Snow?"

"Dominic!" I snapped.

"I'm more comfortable calling you, Mr. Snow." She turned back to her computer. "Ms. Dudeck is sending me a list of possible bands. We're splitting it up. I should get to work making calls."

Chapter 4

Aleena

Valentine's Day was cold, bitterly cold.

I shivered as I cracked the door and glanced outside and then down at my dress.

Fawna and I had butted heads more than once during our shopping excursion last month and most of it had been over the formal dresses, but I had to admit, she'd been right.

Lately, I was coming to realize there was little of which Fawna *wasn't* right.

Now, I wished she would have decided I needed some sort of formal overcoat or cloak and...penguin suit? Just what did a woman wear outside when it was freezing?

The wind was going to tear me to pieces. But I'd just have to suck it up. Easing the door shut, I hurried into the bedroom and checked my appearance one last time.

I'd been both dreading and anticipating this day. Now that it was here, I thought the dread was about to overtake me and I'd end up on my knees, puking my guts up.

Today wasn't just Valentine's Day and it wasn't just kicking off the opening of Dominic's match-making service.

Fawna's last day had been yesterday and I was now, officially, Dominic Snow's personal assistant. And officially, the two of us weren't really talking.

Okay, there wasn't really anything *official* about it, but things had been tense between us for the past week and a half, ever since that mess with the party planner. Fawna had told me that the original party planner had sort of fallen through—as in ended up in rehab. It was being kept quiet, but while Dominic had thought he could handle it on his own, Fawna had squashed that idea. *The man has no idea what goes into planning a party of this magnitude. If he ever attempts to have you organize anything for more than fifteen people, put your foot down and say no. Get a party planner. I always did and if you're firm, he'll do it.*

I would definitely be firm.

I'd had enough headaches just throwing birthday parties back at my dad's old restaurant for groups of ten or twenty. People really don't get how much work goes into that sort of thing—it's a job in and of itself. I didn't need another one on top of...well, Fawna had called herself Dominic's babysitter and I was starting to understand why.

Not that I'd be dealing with Dominic much tonight. I'd be helping the household manager, Janice, while she stayed on top of the staff, and attending to a million other little things.

Dominic was simply here to shine.

But I still got to go to the ball.

Amused with myself, I studied my reflection.

One thing about my heritage, it had gifted me with excellent features. I might have hated them growing up, but I'd come to accept the light brown skin and the gold-streaked brown curls as I'd gotten older.

I'd selected a red dress—why not? It was Valentine's Day, after all. It was a deep, seductive red, but the cut itself was almost conservative, ankle length with a slit up one side that went to just above my knee. It had cap sleeves and a modest neckline, although it still managed to make the most of my assets. The necklace I'd received from my grandmother hung around my neck, resting between my breasts.

I smoothed my hand down the skirt once more, smiling a little at the sight of my white opera gloves glowing against the red silk of the skirt.

"Okay, Cinderella," I murmured. "It's time to go."

I wasn't going to find Prince Charming tonight—and probably not any other night—but wasn't half the fun of it just going to the ball?

I left my bedroom, turning off the lights as I went. I hadn't quite made it to the door when I heard the knock. Frowning, I hurried to the door and checked the peephole, looking out to see Dominic waiting on the porch.

He was facing away, but I'd know him anywhere. Those golden curls, the set of his shoulders...

I opened the door. "Dom..." I corrected myself. "Mr. Snow."

A muscle pulsed in his jaw. "May I come in?"

I hovered there. I didn't really want him in my space. "Is everything okay? I was just leaving. I have to grab my bag—it has my phone. If I need to take care of something—"

"Damn it, Aleena, let me in," he said, pushing past me.

The cold wind sliced into me and I closed the door, shivering as goosebumps broke out over my arms.

Turning to face him, I readied myself for whatever had gone wrong, but he had moved deeper into the house. I found him standing in front of the cold fireplace, staring down into it.

"I need to apologize to you."

Stiffening, I turned away. My little purse, just big enough for my phone, lay on the counter. "Hardly necessary, Mr. Snow. You were right to criticize me as you felt my performance was lacking. Now, we really should be going—"

The rest of the words froze in my throat, then faded, as he brought his hands down on my shoulders. "Stop, Aleena. And for fuck's sake, stop calling me, Mr. Snow."

"Yes, sir." Then I squeezed my eyes shut. *Yes, sir...fuck me, sir...*

Immediately, images of what I'd seen—Dominic bringing the flat of his hand down on Maya's ass, Dominic driving his cock into her waiting body. *Yes, sir...fuck me, sir...*

"Aleena..." My name sounded terribly loud on his lips.

I pulled away from him. Needing room, I strode into the kitchen and pulled down a glass from the counter. After filling it with water, I took a slow, careful sip. "Mr. Snow—" I began.

"Dominic!"

I slammed the glass down with so much force, it was a wonder it didn't break.

"I'm your employee!" I said quietly, forcing myself not to snarl. "I'm not your slave, your toy, a thing, or an idiot. And for the record, this *is* my home—while I'm in your employ. It's *my* legal residence, which means you don't get to come barging in. I'd appreciate some modicum of respect."

He went to say something and I jerked up my hand, cutting him off. "Please, let me finish. I realize I'm only your employee, but surely even employees are worth that much courtesy."

"Surely." His tone was remote, the angle of his head austere.

It was enough to send a shiver down my spine, but I couldn't tell if it was nerves...or something else. Forcing myself to continue, I folded my hands in front of me. "You want to flirt with a woman to get her to do what you want, that is *fine...Mr. Snow*. To my recollection, I don't *think* I made any sort of comment or laughed or did anything unprofessional. However, I did *something* that displeased you. I'm trying to stay professional so I keep my job. Now, either fire me or tell me what I did, but would you *please* stop going from one extreme to the other because you are giving me whiplash!"

He stood in front of me, his face like stone, the only sign of life was the flicker in his eyes. "Are you done?"

I reached for the water and took a sip. I'd splashed some of it on my gloves. I could see the faint little marks on the silk left by the water. I took another sip and then sent him a cool look. "I'm done."

"Good." He took another step toward me. "I'm sorry. I was..." He looked away, staring at the counter over my head for a long moment. Finally, he looked back at me, his eyes solemn. "You're right. This is your home and I shouldn't have forced my way in, so I also owe you an apology for that. I'm sorry. About the matter with the party planner, I was letting a personal issue get in the way and I took it out on you and Fawna. Sometimes, I can be an ass. I have no intention of firing you. You clearly have no problems recognizing when I'm being an ass—you've seen it this past week and you've behaved admirably. You actually should have just told me I was being an ass."

Sniffing, I looked away. "You're my employer. That's not my place."

"I'm making it your place."

From the corner of my eye, I saw him reach up. I tried to brace myself for his touch, but it was impossible.

He trailed his hand down my arm, his fingers grazing my skin. "I'm sorry."

That light touch sent a shiver down my spine. I edged away and rubbed at my arms, pretending to shiver again.

"You're cold."

"It's cold outside," I replied.

"I...yes." He sighed.

The sound was...strangely desolate. Empty, somehow. I slid him a look and saw that he was looking at something. I followed his gaze. He noticed and held up the item in his hand.

It was a mask.

"It's for you, Ms. Davison." His tone was formal.

I'm going to regret this, I thought. "Aleena," I said quietly as I held out my hand for the mask.

He studied me and then moved behind me. "If I may?"

39

"Why do I need this?" I asked as he lifted the mask and settled it into place.

"It's a masquerade...Aleena." His voice was rougher than normal and I closed my eyes, swallowing around the ache that came to my throat.

This was torture. I was starting to think I'd be better off if he *did* fire me.

"But I'm just helping..."

He turned me around and studied me, lifting my chin to angle my head back.

"Come." He held out his arm. "It's almost time for the ball."

"I...um." I cleared my throat and backed away. "I need to get my coat."

***

I didn't take his arm.

I don't know if he noticed—or cared—but he held the door for me and we walked side by side toward the house.

"There's somebody I wanted you to meet before the ball starts," he said as we neared the house. He gave me a look that was decidedly grimmer than it had been a few moments earlier. "Ah...you've talked to her a few times..."

The door swung open before he could finish and I glanced up and then grinned.

"Max!" I climbed the steps and caught the older man around the neck, hugging him. "Don't you look handsome?"

Maxwell had become my regular driver, but I

hadn't expected to see him today. He was clad in a tuxedo rather than his normal suit tie and when he saw me, his face lit up. "Miss Aleena. You looked positively lovely." Then he paused, arching a brow. "That is you, isn't it?"

I laughed. "No. It's Cinderella, silly."

"Ah, yes. Of course. I'll keep an eye out for pumpkins and missing shoes."

"Do shut that door," a cool, cultured voice said. "It's freezing out there."

I turned and found myself facing the very picture of American aristocracy. If such a thing existed...did it?

She looked to be in her early fifties, or perhaps later forties, although I was learning to pick up on the subtle signs of excellent plastic surgery. She was probably in her sixties, but she was absolutely lovely, regardless. Her hair was dark, swept up in an elegant style. As a matter of fact, almost everything about her was elegant.

She stared at me with an arched expression on her face. Somehow, I didn't think introductions were necessary.

Not for me anyway.

"Aleena Davison, this is my mother, Jacqueline St. James-Snow."

"It's nice to meet you." I extended a hand.

She accepted, although I had a feeling it was more out of politeness and obligation. After a light press of her palm to mine, she took her hand back.

"You're replacing Fawna?"

I felt more than saw Dominic stiffen. I gave his mother a polite smile. "No one can replace Fawna. The best I can do is hope to rise to the standard she set."

"Of course." She inclined her head and then turned to Dominic. "I should go out and check the arrangements, make sure your staff has everything under control, Dominic."

"That's Aleena's job, Mom," Dominic said. He glanced at me. "She's perfectly capable of handling it herself. Besides, I want you here with me."

"Of course." I gave them both a polite nod. "Mr. Snow. Mrs. St. James-Snow."

As I walked away, I wondered just what he meant by that. It seemed like their relationship was strained at best, but maybe he just didn't want her wandering around by herself.

I focused on work, heading toward the front of the house. There was a ballroom, small but elegant. In addition to that ballroom, the living room and library had been cleared of furniture, while an elegant buffet had been set up in the formal dining room. There were other public areas as well, a large den, several sitting areas, the oversized foyer and a music room.

I'd wondered if he could possibly fill this huge house, but just the catering staff alone had me shutting down that line of thought. The RSVPs had been flooding in, so my newest worry was where we might *put* all the people who were going to show.

When the guests began to arrive, everything was ready. Fawna was there.

She didn't work for Dominic anymore, but she'd made this one exception.

"My going away party," she told me, snagging a glass of champagne from a passing tray. She asked me if I wanted one and I shook my head.

"You can relax a little," she said. "It's going beautifully."

"I can't drink and work." I shrugged. "I'm a lightweight. You should, though. This is one heck of a going away party."

"Yes." Fawna heaved out a sigh and I don't think it was my imagination that it seemed a little sad. "It certainly is."

Dominic's laugh rang out over the low roar and we both looked up, following the sound. The sadness in her gaze deepened.

Reaching out, I touched her arm. "He's going to be fine."

"I know." She gave me a smile that just ripped at my heart. "He's...Dominic is like the son I never had, Aleena. This hurts."

Then she nudged me between the shoulder blades. "Now, you, pretty young thing, go out there. Dance a little. Live it up."

"I..." I gaped out at the crowd and looked back at her. "I can't!"

"You can." She gave me a sage nod. "Call it a

43

break."

I went to argue and she gave me what I'd come to call her schoolteacher look.

There was no arguing with that. And I knew it.

***

It was the mask, I decided.

Wearing the mask made it so much easier to move among these people.

I'd been watching how everybody acting—not just tonight, but over the past three weeks. I put it into practice now, how they spoke and moved, their mannerisms.

But not their actions.

Maybe I'd pull a chameleon and pretend to fit in. I'd been doing *that* all my life, but I would never be one of these people who smiled at your face and then cut you off the moment your back was turned.

Still, when a man caught my eye and then my hand and proceeded to flirt with me, I was more than a little surprised, then...delighted. I started to smile, then flirt back.

The mask was surprisingly freeing.

Nobody here knew who I was, just a girl from small-town Iowa. They saw a woman in a lovely dress who moved with confidence and poise.

Fake it until you make it, I told myself.

"May I have this dance?"

I glanced up to meet a pair of dark eyes, hidden behind a mask of ivory silk. It glowed against deep brown skin and I felt my lips bowing up in a smile. I almost said yes. It would have been nice, I thought, to see what it was like, to spin across a floor in the arms of a man who found me attractive.

Back home, I'd been the oddball, the geek...the freak. *Ugly fat whore* had come up once or twice, too, after my one, miserable attempt at dating. Yeah, that hadn't gone well.

But as he stood there waiting, his hand outstretched and a smile on his handsome face, I shook my head. "I can't. I'm sorry."

"Another time," he murmured and then retreated into the crowds.

"I think you might have broken his heart," Dominic said.

"I..."

I licked my lips and went to step aside.

But he caught me around the waist and then lifted my hand. "Fawna sent me to dance with you." The music began to play and my breath caught as he dipped his head to murmur in my ear, "Do you know how to waltz?"

"I...ah, yes." I managed a weak smile. "My mom and dad loved to go ballroom dancing, so they taught me. It's been a very long time, though. I was just a kid."

"Just follow me."

"You can find a better partner."

"No." He drew me in closer and the shock of his body so close to mine was almost more than I could handle. "I couldn't. Besides...I'm following orders.

And you're following me."

We started to move and it wasn't long before the familiarity of the moves came back to me. I'd never confess it to anybody, but Dad and I used to waltz around the basement. I'd loved dancing and thought, maybe, for a while, I'd pursue it, but it hadn't ever happened.

"For someone who hasn't waltzed since she was a child," Dominic said. "You do it very well."

"Thank you." I managed to smile. "You can tell Fawna you did your duty."

"Not all of it." A slow grin curled his lips. "She also said you're to take the rest of the evening off. You've worked hard all day and since this is her going-out party, she's going to enjoy it."

His palm flexed on my back, that subtle movement sending a shiver up my spine. There was no way I could pretend I was cold, not as warm as it was in here with all the bodies swaying to the music.

You're so beautiful, I thought, darting a glance up at his features, partially concealed behind the simple mask. So beautiful.

He watched me expectantly and I looked away, unable to think of anything to say.

Maybe it was that beautiful face that left me feeling so tongue-tied.

A soft sigh escaped him and I glanced back at him. Our eyes connected and I felt like I was falling, drowning, lost in the depths of his eyes. That's what it was. His eyes left me feeling mesmerized.

46

They left me weak.

"You look lovely tonight, Aleena," he said, his voice barely loud enough to be heard above the music.

Uncertain what to say, I just smiled and focused on the diamond—and I was sure it was a diamond—that winked at me from the small pin on his lapel.

"Are you still angry with me?"

"No." I swung my gaze back up to his just as he moved me into a quick spin. It left my heart racing and I was breathless by the time I looked back at him. "No, I'm not angry."

"Then why aren't you speaking to me?"

"It's...loud," I said lamely, shrugging.

"It was loud earlier, but I saw you talking to Fawna."

The song ended and I started to pull away, but he tightened his grip on my waist, sensing my need to escape, but unwilling to let go.

The next song that began was a slow song, low and smooth, sexy as hell. I couldn't have named the singer for the life of me, but every time I heard it, from now until the end of my life, I'd remember this. The way he felt as he drew me in even closer, the way it felt as he caught my right hand and drew it up to the back of his neck.

"I should go," I said, my voice rasping.

"You're not working anymore tonight," he said as he brought one hand down to the base of my spine. It rested there, burning through the silk of my dress. The other slowly slid up and down my back, a touch that was strangely soothing and sensual at the same time.

I could feel his hair tickling my wrists and I resisted the urge to run my fingers through the golden strands. I looked away and stared out into the sea of bodies, all of them swaying to the music.

"Well, I guess you're happy with how your ball is going."

"Yes." The deep, guttural tone of his voice, so close to my ear, had me turning my head to look at him.

That was my mistake. He'd bent his head to speak to me. Now, with our mouths so closed together, we froze.

I licked my lips.

I had one split second to think, *Move, Aleena!*

And then somebody moved, alright.

But it wasn't me.

The hand on my back slid up, cupping the back of my neck. I gasped as his mouth covered mine, firm and hard and striking soft at the same time. His tongue slid out, flicking at the seam of my lips and I gasped.

Then, I twisted away.

Immediately, Dominic's hands fell away.

He gazed at me with cool composure. "Thank you for the dance, Aleena. Happy Valentine's Day."

He turned on his heel and walked away.

Chapter 5

Dominic

She tasted like temptation.

Brooding, I stared into the scotch I'd poured.

I no longer wanted the liquor.

It had been stupid, kissing her like that. It had been stupid, dancing with her like that. Stupid...and I'd do it all over again.

The past week had been lousy, even though the Valentine's party had been a huge success, launching *Trouver L'Amour* to the masses. While I should have been celebrating, I'd been distracted. I'd been worried about Aleena taking the job because she seemed so...not right. Innocent and sweet, yes, but she didn't move in my world and when you were a cute little guppy swimming among the sharks, you tended to get eaten—fast.

But she wasn't a guppy.

She was sweet, yes, and definitely innocent, but

there was more spine to her than I'd imagined. More steel, too. I can't think of too many people, other than Fawna and a few select members of my management who would have stood up to me the way she had. I guess that was what Fawna had seen in her, but it had caught me off-guard.

She was turning out to be perfect for the PA job. And hell on my state of mind.

Now I knew how she tasted.

I wanted to see how she felt, stretched out under me, bent over before me.

I wanted to see what she looked like, those long, toned limbs tied over her head and I wanted to see that ass lifted for me as I drove inside her.

I wanted to feel the curve of her rump as I spanked her and I wanted to feed her my cock until she couldn't take any more.

I was starting to crave it.

I'm not your slave, I'm not your toy...

Swearing, I tossed back the scotch and rested my head against the back of my chair. The problem was, when it came to women, that was about all the use I had for them.

Not a true slave, not really. There were relationships in the world I lived in that went that far, yeah, but they *were* relationships. After the hell I'd lived through, the last thing I wanted was to have complete and total control over a person, even if they willingly gave it.

But submission?

I needed that.

It was the only way I could find pleasure most of the time. I needed it, craved it like a drug and sometimes, it still wasn't enough to silence the screams in my head.

I'm not your thing!

Shoving upright, I spun away and threw the crystal tumbler I held into the wall.

It splintered and fell to the ground in shards.

I didn't see her as a thing. Which was part of the problem. She was starting to be too real to me already.

***

A face swam before my eyes.

I struggled, tried to move—couldn't.

"What do you want...who are you!" I shouted. My voice shook and I hated myself.

He sat down.

Fear lurched inside me. A man I didn't know was standing over me.

"You should let me go," I said after a minute. "My parents. They got money. They'll find you and hunt you down."

Now there was a smile on his face, an ugly one. The man grabbed my face, bent over me and laughed.

"Rich, are they? Find me?"

I tried to jerk away, but I was tied up, tied down—couldn't escape. No escape...words started to echo in my head. No release. No ransom. No rescue.

Panicked, I tore at my restraints. *No, no, no...*

The man was big—like the size of a room big and I tried again, and again, and again...I couldn't get away...could I?

Then I was on my ass, sliding across the floor as a monster stalked me.

"There will be no release. No ransom." He gestured to the bed and just like that, I was bound again, restrained, unable to move.

"This is how it's going to work..."

He started to talk.

And I started to scream...

***

"Dominic!"

Someone was shaking me.

Too many months of forced imprisonment had left a mark and I came up ready to fight. I caught my attacker and reacted, pinning him—

No...her.

Aleena.

"Aleena," I whispered, sucking in a breath.

She stared up at me with wide, scared eyes. Her hands were on my shoulders still, but now they were pushing at me, as if in fear.

Slowly, I caught one wrist. Then the other.

"Aleena..."

"You..." She licked her lips.

The sight of her tongue sliding along her lips did me in. I had to stop thinking. I had to. With the dregs of the dream still dragging me down, I crushed my mouth to hers.

Chapter 6

Aleena

Earlier in the evening

What were you thinking?

What was Dominic *thinking?*

My mind swung between those two questions on a crazy seesaw that kept me from sleeping. Worse, when I lay in my bed, trying to sleep, I'd close my eyes and imagine that night from a few weeks ago.

Maya tied to the bed, her butt pink from Dominic's hand, but now, instead of Maya's long, pale body, it was my shorter, rounder one.

I could see him grabbing my hair and pulling my head back, kissing me...and now I had his taste, imprinted on my memory.

Yes, sir...

"What were you thinking?" I muttered. And *again*, what had *he* been thinking?

I loved my new job—usually. But this was going to mess up, I knew it. It was bad enough I'd seen my boss having sex, bad enough I was attracted to him, but now?

When it had just been my dirty little secret, watching him with Maya, it hadn't been so bad. That had been...fantasy. Two people—people who weren't *me*. The kiss, though. That was real.

Lying in my bed as the clock crept past three, then four, I finally gave up trying to sleep and climbed out of bed.

I thought I'd get some work done and automatically reached for my phone, only to cringe. I'd left it back at the main house in the kitchen. I'd been afraid I'd put it down somewhere and lose it, and then I'd up and left without it.

I had my laptop and could easily work from it, but I felt lost without the phone. It was easy to see why so many people complained of being addicted to their phones now.

Sighing, I looked down at the yoga pants and tank top I'd slept in and then stood up. At least I wasn't trekking out there in a silk formal this time. But I had to have my phone.

After donning a coat, gloves and scarf, I headed outside. My breath was visible and each inhale was cold enough to hurt my throat. By the time I managed to get the key into the lock, my fingers were numb.

I stepped inside, shivering as the heat from the house began to warm me. It took a moment for my eyes to adjust, but I didn't turn on a light. There were small hall and room lights scattered throughout the entire house to keep it from being pitch black and that was fine with me. If I turned on the main lights, there was the chance Dominic would see the lights and come down to investigate.

I so wasn't ready to see him.

I shoved my gloves into my pockets and stepped out of the boots, a habit I'd developed in childhood—*don't track your mess in, Aleena!*

Absently, I glanced up and saw that the staff had already done a light cleaning, although a morning crew would be in to give the house a thorough cleaning starting at seven. Pierson, the butler who handled things here at the house—had gone over all these details with me and the chef, Mary, several times over.

The house was almost eerily quiet.

In the dead of night, most places are. I glanced toward the doors that led to the rooms at the back of the house where most of the on-site staff slept. A place this big needed staff on-site around the clock and I didn't want to wake anybody.

Easing the drawer open, I pulled out the little purse I'd bought for my phone and took it out.

I checked it and saw that I'd missed a couple of calls, but nothing important. Sighing, I slid the phone into my coat and turned to go.

A long, low noise echoed through the house.

I froze, heat rushing up my cheeks as I remembered the last time I'd heard a strange noise in this place.

Not again, I told myself.

But as I went to put on my boots, I heard it again.

That...no. That wasn't right.

A second later, the noise became a scream, a tortured one of pain.

I took off running.

I heard it again and in my gut, I knew who it was.

Dominic.

I wrenched open the door knob and shoved it open, staring in, uncertain what I'd find.

Sucking in a breath, I stared at the moonlight streaming down in the bed, centered under a massive skylight.

Dominic...?

He twisted on the bed, a harsh noise escaping him. A wordless sort of denial.

Shrugging out of my coat, I let it fall to the floor as I went to him.

His sheets were tangled around his waist, but his chest was bare. His arms were moving, as if fending off something or someone. His face was contorted as he made another sound. This one wasn't a yell. It was a whimper.

"Dominic," I said softly, settling my hip on the edge of the bed. He didn't wake. I grabbed his shoulders and tried not to think about the fact that his skin was bare beneath my palms.

"Dominic!" I shook him, then harder when he didn't respond.

Suddenly, his eyes popped open.

I had barely even a second to process it before I was thrown beneath him, his hands gripping my wrists as he pinned me down. Terror blasted through me.

And then, he blinked.

"Aleena," he said, panting.

"I..." My breath wasn't coming any easier than his.

"Aleena..."

Oh shit.

His mouth was hard, desperate, and this time, he didn't seek entrance to my mouth.

He just took it.

Our first kiss had been hot and slow, a tease...a temptation. This one was pure, raw desire, and something primal twisted low in my stomach.

When his hands slid down my back to tug at the back of my shirt, I knew what he wanted.

Fuck it.

I was tired of playing it safe.

I raised my arms and let him pull my shirt off. He came back down on top of me and I wrapped my arms around him, welcoming his weight. I barely processed the fact that he was naked.

I shivered and then his mouth was on me, lips and tongue moving across my collarbones and down to the tops of my breasts. His hands slipped under me, arching me up as he closed his mouth around one nipple, then the other.

I moaned, then, as he tugged on me with his teeth, I whimpered.

I ran my hands up his arms, squeezing as he licked and sucked on the hardening flesh. His teeth teased at it and I whimpered. I ran my hands down his chest, nails raking over his flat nipples until his hands went to my waist. His hand slid past the waistband of my yoga pants as his mouth returned to mine.

I wrapped my arms around his neck, pulling him closer. I pushed my tongue into his mouth, eager to taste and explore. I knew this would never happen again. I wanted to make the most of it. I curled my tongue around his and then started to shudder as he slid a finger between my folds, stroking it over my clit.

Hot waves of pleasure blasted at me and I tensed, shudders wracking my entire body. I could feel his cock hard against my hip. I arched up against him as he nipped at my bottom lip. His lips traced down over my jaw to my throat and his hand moved lower.

When he pushed one finger inside me, I cried out.

"So tight," he murmured against the side of my neck.

I raised my hips to meet his hand. His teeth raked along my neck, adding to the sensation racing through me. Heat built inside and I tensed beneath him, nails biting into his skin.

Dominic's teeth scraped against the place where my neck and shoulder met and I whimpered. He pulled skin into his mouth as a second finger joined the first. He wasn't gentle as he pumped his fingers into me, twisting and curling, rubbing against me, sending hot sparks of pleasure dancing across my nerves. Then his thumb started flicking across my clit and I was coming.

I choked on a scream as I rode out my orgasm. I felt Dominic's hands on my hips, jerking my pants away.

Panting for air, I stared down, watching as he settled his weight across me once more. I didn't dare look at his face, afraid that any eye contact would break the spell we were under and end this.

I didn't want it to end, not yet.

He came between my legs, the head of his cock rubbing against me. My heart thudded against my ribs and I whimpered when he passed against me, once, twice.

He propped himself up on one arm and then slowly, he pushed inside. I cried out, unable to silence the noise as he surged against me. When I thought I could take no more, he withdrew and I caught my breath, but then, he retreated and it began again.

He stretched me impossibly wide and pain mixed with pleasure. I squeezed my eyes shut, the sensations overwhelming.

He barely paused when he reached the end of me, drawing back and then surging forward with a primal groan. I grabbed onto his arms as he pounded into me, each stroke harder than the last. It was like nothing I'd ever felt before. Nothing could compare to this.

Dominic dipped his head and rubbed his mouth against mine. At the same time, he slid a hand between us. When his fingers circled around my clit, I clenched down around him.

"Don't...don't do...fuck, fuck, fuck!" he growled as he buried himself inside me.

Abruptly, he came down harder against me, grabbing my hands and forcing them high over my head. Any sound I might have made was caught by his mouth as he kissed me, a savage, demanding claiming as he started to ride me, his body moving higher, stroking against my clit with each driving thrust.

His cock swelled. I felt it within me. Pleasure crashed and swelled and the combined sensations sent me flying. I came hard and fast, even as Dominic's hips jerked against mine.

He swore against my mouth, his teeth sinking into my lower lip with a force that was almost too much, but in that moment, I didn't care.

I only cared about the pressure of his body on mine, the movement...and the sound of my name of his lips.

Endless moments passed as our breathing slowed.

He pulled me close, tugging me up against his body as though he'd never let me go. I might have thought he was still asleep, but he pressed his face into my hair and I heard him murmur my name.

I think I also heard my heart crack.

Right down the middle.

Eventually, he slept.

It wasn't until that moment that I let myself climb out of the bed and dress. I slipped out of the house in silence, hardly daring to think about what I had done.

Chapter 7

Aleena

I awoke sore.

There was a time when I'd woken in this state before, but the memories hadn't been anything like this. That time, I'd been flooded with shame and misery and regret.

This time?

There was just...wistfulness.

Last night had been a fantasy. A dream. Something that wasn't likely to ever happen again and I knew it, but damn if I wouldn't relish those memories, even if I didn't wonder about the cause behind them.

His nightmare.

I couldn't help but recall the scars I'd seen on Dominic and wonder if the nightmare from last night lay behind whatever had caused those marks on his body. Something had marked him, and not just physically.

I can't claim any great insight, other than instinct, but I'd be willing to bet everything I had that I was right.

Last night, he'd been like a different man, one chased by demons. I could see the echoes of those demons on me even now. The mirror showed the evidence as I dressed, revealing what I hadn't seen in my haste to hide myself in the covers last night.

The hickey on my neck was only one mark.

My hips bore the marks of his hands. My breath catching, I stared at myself, my breath hitching as I recalled how it had felt, to have him driving into me, his breath ragged in my ear.

"Stop it," I told myself. "Just stop."

Averting my gaze, I tugged on a pair of jeans—nice and casual. It was the weekend, after all. I topped the jeans with a pretty blouse and a scarf, hiding the mark on my neck.

I took a little time to deal with my hair and then I brushed on some make-up and glanced at the clock. I'd had four hours of sleep.

Not a lot, but I couldn't lay in bed when I had work to do.

***

I'd thought—*hoped*—that his nightmare, the party, all of it, would allow me some peace.

I hadn't even had five minutes inside the house before he found me. Leaning against the counter, whittling down the task list for the day, I nibbled on toast and guzzled coffee and had absolutely no time to brace myself.

One moment I was alone.

The next...

"Aleena." His tone was soft and heat bloomed in my stomach.

Slowly, I lowered my cup of coffee. He stood in the doorway.

Behind him, organized chaos reigned. Pierson and Co—as I'd taken to calling the staff at the main house—were out in full force. Already, they'd made a significant dent and it wasn't even eight in the morning.

Oddly enough, it was their presence that gave me some modicum of control.

I sipped at my sugar-laden coffee and smiled at Dominic over the rim. I was pleased with the professional slant of said smile, too. "Good morning, Dominic."

"I think we need to talk."

I glanced past him into the hall and then looked down at the phone I had just put down, at my agenda, pursing my lips. My heart skipped a beat, but he didn't need to know that. Nor did he need to know how the sight of him standing there in worn jeans and a battered T-shirt made him look completely and totally biteable.

"Oh?" I glanced at him and then took a sip of my coffee. "Was there something on the agenda for the day? I'm going to be pretty slammed getting everything in order after last night, but I should be able to free up some time within the next few hours."

Denial, as they say, isn't just a river in Egypt.

He scowled at me and then reached out and flipped my phone over. "Fuck the agenda. *We* need to talk."

A knot lodged in my throat as I slanted a look up at him. The expression on his face was one I hadn't seen before. Concern...and the slightest edge of panic.

Abruptly, I understood.

I was his employee.

We worked together, and more than that, we had a weird set of living arrangements. I could only imagine where his thoughts were traveling. I drew in a deep, slow breath, preparing myself to say something—anything.

He beat me to it.

"I am so sorry about last night. I don't know what got into me. I never—"

"It's okay." I plastered a smile I didn't feel on my face. The last thing I needed to hear was that I wasn't his type, that we didn't move in the same worlds, or that he hadn't meant any of it and that it had been a mistake. I *knew* all of that.

"No, it's not!" A bit of his control slipped. "We didn't...I mean, I didn't..." He ran a hand through his hair. "Damn it!"

"Okay." I ran my tongue across my teeth and put down my cup of coffee. Crossing my arms over my chest, I studied him. "Why don't you just tell me what's on your mind, Dominic?"

He gave me a puzzled look, as if he couldn't figure out why I was being so calm. "I don't know what you remember about last night, but we didn't use any protection."

Oh, that. I looked away and hoped my flush didn't show. "Yeah. I'm aware."

"I am so sorry," he repeated. "I don't know what came over me. I know better. And you shouldn't worry about anything. I get tested every couple months, just in case and I always use protection." He paused, and then added in a wry voice, "Or at least it used to be always."

I really was an idiot, I thought. Nausea pitched and rolled through me, but I'd deal with that later. Looking away, I jerked a shoulder in a shrug. "You...look. I didn't think about it either. You don't have anything to worry about on my end. I'm clean."

"It's not..." He swore. "Damn it, Aleena. It's not just that. I know better."

"I'm twenty-one years old," I snapped, shooting him a dark look. "I've been aware of what sex—and the consequences—are for quite a while. So technically, *I* know better, too."

He sucked in a breath, then stopped. "Okay. Okay. Look, I'll have Maxwell drive you to the pharmacy in town. Plan B is covered by your insurance—"

"No." I sucked in a breath as I realized just where his train of thought had gone.

Plan B. So that's what this is about. He was freaking out because he was worried he might have knocked me up. Turning around, I picked up my coffee and stared out over the lavish gardens.

"Relax, boss. I'm on the pill." I fell back into matter-of-fact, professional mode. That explained things. Bad enough to fuck an employee, but to knock one up would've been worse.

I mentally thanked Molly for persuading me to go on the pill four months ago.

"You are now dating and condoms are not hundred percent safe," she'd insisted.

Dating...

It was the only guy I'd dated since moving to Manhattan and it'd been a disaster. He'd turned out to be a complete prick but thankfully I found out before sleeping with him. I was still on the pill, however.

I fought not to cringe as I heard Dominic heave out a sigh of relief.

All that panic, I thought dismally. Apparently, the thought of having a baby with a woman like me was just too hideous for him to comprehend.

Casually, I gathered up my dishes and moved to the sink. "There's nothing to concern yourself about, sir. It was a heat of the moment thing. Neither one of us was expecting what happened."

I turned to face him, ready to excuse myself, but that just didn't seem to be in the cards. Dominic cleared his throat, shifting his weight uneasily. "Okay. Well...yeah..."

He cleared his throat, looking humiliated as he turned away. "Now that we've gotten that out of the way..." He went to the refrigerator and took out an energy drink. "We really should talk about what happened."

No. I mentally shook my head at the very thought of it. I wasn't going to do this. Maybe that was crazy—weren't guys the ones who were supposed to be resistant to the idea of *talking* about things? As I stood there, feeling awkward and uncertain, I realized that *I* was the one who didn't want to talk about this. I didn't want to have the emotions I was already feeling for him laid bare.

Clearing my throat, I said, "Look, Dominic, last night was a fluke."

It was the truth and I knew, but admitting it made it no less painful. I forced myself to smile, like it was no big deal. But it was...and it hurt.

As I spoke, his brows shot up, but Dominic said nothing.

"I don't know how much you remember," I said, turning away before I could read the answer on his face. I didn't want to know what he really thought about last night. "I came into the house because I'd forgotten my phone. I heard a noise from upstairs and thought you were in trouble." I kept things simple. "It looked like you were having a nightmare of some kind."

"You woke me up," he said softly. "I remember where things went from there."

I shrugged. "Like I said...it was a fluke. It was the heat of the moment. Neither of us was thinking clearly."

"Aleena."

No. I wasn't going to think about the way he said my name. It didn't mean anything special. Not to him.

"It didn't mean anything," I said. The words almost came out harsh. "I'm not expecting anything from you. I don't think we're in a relationship and I'm not going to accuse you of sexual harassment." I turned slightly and gave him the best smile I could. "No blackmail, or lawsuits. It was just sex. End of."

"Just sex."

I looked over at him. His expression was blank.

Silence stretched out, and then after a moment, he cleared his throat. "Okay." He took a drink and then continued, "Okay, look...yeah, last night complicated things. For the record, I never assumed you would try and accuse me of harassment, although..." He turned away and braced his hands on the counter. "If you did, you'd probably have a case. I put my hands on you, Aleena. We both know it."

"Yeah, well, I didn't knock them off," I muttered.

He glanced at me through his lashes.

I glared back.

After a moment, he looked away. "I'm sorry. It

shouldn't have happened."

"Agreed." I inclined my head.

He nodded. "I don't do this. I don't do relationships and complications. With anyone, especially not an employee."

"That sounds..." *Lonely*, I thought. "Wise." Then I smiled at him. "Stop worrying. We're good. We've got a working relationship and believe me, that's all I want."

He smiled at me, that polite, professional smile that I was sure made a lot of women swoon. But I'd seen his real smile, the one that made his eyes light up. This one was only a shadow compared to the other.

Chapter 8

Dominic

I'd seriously fucked up.

I knew that if I told Fawna what I'd done, she'd not only agree with me, she'd probably slap me upside the back of my head for doing something that stupid. The kiss at the ball had been dumb enough, but what happened that night was even worse.

But to be honest, my mistakes had started far earlier than that. It had started almost the moment I'd seen her standing at the door of my penthouse.

It had gotten worse over the past few weeks and had culminated last night. The moment I'd had her in my arms, I'd known I'd made a mistake. She'd fit there perfectly, as if we'd been made to dance together.

That accidental kiss that hadn't been as accidental as I'd made it out to be...if I'd just not done that, then maybe I would have been okay.

But I told myself if I tasted her, if I tried that

sweet mouth, I'd see that she wasn't as sweet, wasn't everything I was hoping, thinking...

And I'd been right.

She was more.

Just sex.

She was wrong. I'd had plenty of *just sex*—so I should know.

Two weeks since it had happened and I couldn't stop thinking about it. I stared at my computer screen without really seeing what was on it. My concentration had been shot for the past few weeks, ever since the night Aleena and I had slept together.

Aleena had proven to be a godsend, there to help me smooth out the bumps and hurdles that came with any new business. She had a head for this. I loved business and the business of making money, but the organization required was something I loathed.

Aleena, though, she just might turn out to surpass Fawna. She was organized in every way I wasn't and she could follow-up on things I never thought of until I didn't realize I'd need them. My life was already flowing smoother.

And yet...it wasn't.

Sex was easy—and terrible as it sounds—forgettable. Usually. Although it had been over two weeks, I hadn't forgotten Aleena.

Needing to get away from her, I'd told her last night I had a project I needed her to take care of and I'd pointed her in the direction of my home office.

It was, in a word, chaos.

Fawna rarely ventured inside unless she had to and since most of the business matters I needed dealt with could be done via email or through our synced calendars, she didn't have to very often.

Life was easier that way—for her and for me, because I didn't want to listen to her bitch about how disorganized I was and she didn't have to listen to me bitch about how I didn't need my home office to be neat. I didn't need to impress anybody there. That was the one place I didn't have to be in control or worry.

But it would keep Aleena busy and I could have a chance to think. It would also give me a chance to be away from her without thinking about how her hair had felt in my hands, how soft her body had been under mine and how her pussy had felt, clutching at my dick as I drove deep inside her.

It had been a wasted effort.

Even here, in the offices of *Trouver L'Amour*, I hadn't been able to get away from her. Even now, with Valentine's Day behind us and March breathing down my neck, several clients were curious about my *enchanting* dance partner and a few people had congratulated me on the publicity stunt.

There was a buzz and I looked up, pushed the speaker on my phone. "Yes?"

"Mr. Snow, you have a call from Jefferson Sinclair."

Immediately, my black mood plummeted even

more. I almost told my administrative assistant to tell him I was out, but she'd done that twice already and I suspected he'd keep calling. He'd emailed twice, too.

"Thanks, Amber. I'll take the call."

I pinched the bridge of my nose and then snagged the phone.

"Hey, Jefferson. How are you doing, man?"

"Dominic!" Jefferson's voice, deep and smooth, came through the phone. He belonged to that dreaded *new money* crowd, but in a move that appalled my family, Jefferson and I had become friends. His father had been district attorney up until he'd had a heart attack and it was entirely likely Jefferson would follow in his footsteps—the attorney part only, I hoped.

"What can I do for you, Jefferson? I'm pretty tight on time these days, trying to get this new business up and going."

"That, my friend, is why I'm calling." Jefferson didn't waste a moment. "The woman—that angel you had on the dance floor. Please tell me you're not involved and please tell me you can introduce me. If she's a client, then sign me up."

"Ah..."

Something came through in my voice.

Jefferson hesitated and then asked, "Are you involved?"

"No," I said after a moment. "No, we're not."

"But..." Jefferson blew out a breath. "Okay.

Sounds like you want something to be there."

I pushed back from my desk and moved to the window. "I don't know what I want."

"Dom, when have you ever?"

Closing my eyes, I said, "That's not the issue. Look, I can't help you out with this, but if you're wanting to sign on here, I can—"

"Nah, man." Jefferson cut me off. "The party was amazing and it sounds like you've got a good thing going, not that I'm surprised. You're like Midas. But I barely have time to sleep these days and you know how half your crowd sees me. I'm that uppity lawyer who has the balls to think I've got the right to sit at your table."

I laughed, but there wasn't much humor in it.

"I'd rather neither of us sit at that table. It's a pain in the ass," I told him.

"Fine. We'll head back to my dad's old neighborhood and find us some real food— something that's meant to be eaten, not just sit on a plate and look pretty. And maybe you can tell me about this woman of yours."

"She's not mine, Jefferson." That admission caused a pang every time I thought it.

"You sure about that?"

Before I could answer, he had another call come in. "Okay, rich boy," Jefferson said. "I gotta go. Been waiting on that call. Listen, you drop me a line if you feel like getting together."

He was gone before I had a chance to say

anything else.

Dropping the phone into the cradle, I braced my hands on the table.

She's not mine.

You sure about that?

Yeah. I was sure. But I sure as hell *wanted* her to be mine.

I could feel her skin under my fingers, against my tongue. It had been so soft, like silk. And the way it had felt to sink inside her...

"Damn it!"

Tired of fighting it, I dropped down on the couch and leaned back, staring up at the ceiling.

She wasn't mine. Wouldn't ever be mine.

But if she was...

There was nothing about her I didn't like. That core of steel, her humor, the kindness.

And now...groaning, I slid a hand down my chest and cupped myself through the fine wool of my trousers.

I'd entertained a few fantasies of her submitting to me, her low, velvety soft voice rough with need as she said, *'Yes, sir'*.

She'd submit. One night in bed—no, after that first kiss, I'd known. Maybe that was why I'd been so stupid. I'd been around her long enough to get a rough idea and the thought of it had been slowly driving me crazy, but now I knew. When you've been in this lifestyle as long as I have, you start to develop an eye for it.

She'd never fully embrace the life of submission, but I didn't need that.

I didn't want a woman who'd let me take her over—I'd *been* taken over.

But I wanted a woman who'd give herself up to me. Who'd yield.

That's what dominance was about after all. The trust of it, the yielding. A woman—or a man—trusting their dominant enough to yield. I wanted that from Aleena. I wanted her to trust me and yield and give herself over.

I could almost picture her on her knees, chin up but eyes down, her breasts rising and falling with each breath.

I wished I'd turned on the light that night so I could've seen every inch of her. I knew the feel and the taste and the shape of her nipples, but I didn't know the color. I knew she had a neat patch of curls between her thighs—I usually made my lovers wax, but I hadn't minded with Aleena. Now I wanted to see those curls, to spread her open and lick her, clean her, then make her wet all over again.

More than that, I wished I would've taken my time with her.

I wanted to see her on her knees, wanted to watch that pretty mouth part around my cock, watch as she took me as deep as she could and then I'd work with her until she could take me deeper. I wanted to teach her to take my cock into her throat.

My stomach clenched and my cock grew even

harder. I swore and the words came out low and rough.

I imagined it was Aleena's hands on me. I shouldn't be thinking about her this way. Wondering what it would be like to introduce Aleena to my lifestyle. Seeing those wide, innocent eyes looking up at me while I fucked her mouth. Watching how her light golden skin flushed with pink as I spanked her or used a flogger.

I imagined bringing her to the edge, then taking her over. Holding her as she calmed. Would she cry? The first few times a dominant brought a sub to the edge could be emotional—even beyond those first few times, it could be emotional. I'd had more than a few women cry after...

After.

Swallowing, I rose from the couch and started to pace.

I didn't like to think about after. I was considered to be a *kind* dominant, even though I'd gotten more selective. I wasn't looking to be a therapist and if I suspected any sub I was interested in was as fucked up as I was, then I looked for...calmer pastures.

But it didn't always happen.

Sometimes, a woman cried in my arms and when it ended, I felt like an ass when I bundled her up and send her home with my driver. Very few people drove in New York and I sure as hell wasn't putting a partner of mine into a taxi if she was going through some serious emotional upheaval.

Aleena had been the one to hold me, though. And there would be no cabs, no drivers. She lived with me—or at least, she lived under my roof or on my property.

Agitated, when my cellphone rang, I grabbed it, thinking a call would distract me and I could stop thinking about this, even if only for a few minutes.

I realized a second after I'd answered what a mistake that had been.

"Hello, Mom."

Chapter 9

Aleena

After two weeks, you'd think I could forget about that night.

Or at least put it up on a shelf—like a keepsake.

A hot, sexy, torrid, it-really-shouldn't-have-happened keepsake. I sighed. But it had happened, so I needed to-deal-with-it sort of keepsake.

It didn't work, though.

The only thing that halfway kept me from reliving it over and over was work—as in working nonstop.

Fortunately, there was plenty to keep me busy.

Dominic was constantly throwing more work at me, from cleaning the office at the penthouse, *then* the office at the main house and when that was all done, he had me start digging up information on a business down in Philadelphia.

But as busy as I was, even when I fell down face-first into exhaustion, I couldn't keep myself from dreaming.

More than once, I'd woken up breathing heavily, my heart racing. Sometimes, I would wake up, my hand inside my panties and I'd roll over and muffle my moans into my pillow.

He was my boss. I lived with him. What had happened was in the past and it had been a mistake. Momentary weakness brought on by sympathy for whatever he'd been going through combined with a bout of homesickness compounded by the loneliness of not having spent much time with Molly.

A trifecta of excuses.

That sounded good enough to keep me from completely freaking out. For the first couple of days at least. As more time passed and the tension between us didn't go away, I started to wonder if I'd completely screwed everything up.

There were times in a girl's life when there are only two things you can reach for—your phone and your wine.

I grabbed one of the bottles I'd picked up—Dominic had been subtly teaching me the finer points of alcohol and I'd fallen in love with Italian wines, especially once I'd figured out how affordable some of them were. Even though I was making a lot more money than before, growing up middle-class had taught me to respect the almighty dollar.

Then I grabbed my Bluetooth. Fawna had told me that I'd grow to love it and she was right.

By the time I hit the kitchen, I had Molly on the

line.

"Aleena!"

I couldn't help but smile. "Hey, Moll."

"Are we still on for next week?"

"Yeah." I'd almost forgotten. Checking my phone, I saw that I still had the note on my calendar, along with a note that I had emailed Dominic and he'd emailed back. I had the weekend off. "I'm not catching you at work, am I?"

Even though she wasn't allowed to have her phone on the floor, I knew Molly didn't always follow the rules, and if she'd seen it was a call from me, she might've answered the phone anyway.

"No," she said. "I have the day off. Worked a double both Saturday and Sunday."

"That sucks," I said as I tugged down a box of pasta. Francisco had told me he could teach me to make fresh pasta, but I'd politely declined. I'd rather spend what little free time I had doing something other than make spaghetti by hand.

"It is what it is," she said breezily. "But I know you didn't call to listen to me complain about work. What's up?"

I took a deep breath. Here it was. I had two choices. I could lie and tell her I'd missed her and just wanted to talk, which wasn't technically a lie since I really had missed her. Or, I could be honest and spill my guts about all that had happened over the past two weeks.

After a moment of a brief but intense internal

debate, I picked the latter. "I did something really stupid."

"Spill." Molly's voice went from carefree to serious in a second.

"When I first met Dominic, I thought he was hot, you know?"

"Well, yeah," she said. "You like guys and have eyes. Not much else needs to be said about that. The man's gorgeous."

"Thing is, Molly, he's not just good-looking."

"He's rich, too," she added.

"Well, yeah...but...look, he's more than that. He's decent to work for. A lot better than Gary, for sure." Then I grimaced. "Not that he can't be an ass, but we all have our moments."

As I put some water on, Molly said, "Get to it, honey. Whatever it is...oh, hell. Are you falling for this guy?"

Silence was my only answer.

"Shit, Aleena, are you falling for him?" she asked again.

I closed my eyes and leaned on the counter. "I don't know, Molly."

She was quiet a moment and then softly, she said, "You know, we can't always pick and choose with this kind of thing, but...do you think that's wise?"

For a moment, I just stared down in the pot of water.

"I don't think I really have much choice," I

whispered.

"Then I think it's past the '*I don't know*' phase, isn't it?"

Frustrated, I turned away from the stove and dug out some olive oil. There was fresh garlic—I *could* figure that part out. "Yeah. I think it is."

"Well..." Molly blew out a breath. "Look, we both know it's a bad idea to get involved with somebody we work with. It gets messy. Things get awkward. But if you don't go sleeping with him—"

"Um, yeah. Well, about that."

"You didn't." I could all but hear Molly shaking her head.

"I...kinda did." I dumped pasta into the now boiling water. "Remember I told you his new company was having this big Valentine's Day party?"

"Yeah, we had to cancel our plans, right?"

"Well, he asked me to dance."

Molly said, "Okay, but please tell me you didn't have a quickie on the floor."

"Ha, ha." As the pasta started to boil, I opened my bottle of wine. "Look...he kissed me. It was...weird. Kinda like we bumped mouths or it was no big deal. But it freaked me out and I left. But I ended up going back to the main house later. I'd forgotten my phone and...anyway. I heard him and...it was this nightmare, Molly. It was something awful. I woke him up and he kissed me and things just kind of went from there."

Molly was quiet for a moment, then she asked,

"Were you careful?"

"No." I had to squeeze the word out. "And now...shit, Moll. Everything's weird. He acts weird, I act weird. Nothing's right anymore."

"No shit," she said. "Okay, first...you're going to go get tested."

"I'm on the pill."

"Not *that* kind of tested."

"But..."

"Don't," Molly said quietly. "I'm sure he's told you he's clean, and I'm pretty sure you are. But you're going to be smart. Don't take a chance, okay? We can go together. You'll probably even feel better for it. Okay?"

Taking a deep breath, I stared at the glass of wine I'd yet to drink. Then I said, "Okay."

"Okay. Now...second, and here's the big Q. Do you like him?"

"I do," I admitted. "I just don't know what it means because what happened between the two of us can never happen again, so what's the point?"

"But what if you can?"

"But Molly..." My heart constricted. "I'm just...me."

"Yeah. You're you and you're awesome. Why can't you have the prince?"

I started to shake my head, then stopped. "It's more complicated than that."

"Why? Because he's rich? Fuck the money. If he's this great guy like you're telling me, the only

90

thing that should matter is whether or not he likes you back."

But there's more to it.

I wasn't about to explain the kind of things Dominic was into, not on the phone. And after that night, he probably knew...oh *fuck*.

"Molly," I whispered, humiliation crowding up into me. "What if..." I had to stop and take a drink of the wine just to continue, "...what if I was just so bad in bed...I mean, it's not like I've got much experience, you know? What if I was so lousy and that's why he doesn't want to talk to me now?"

"Bullshit." Molly didn't even pause before the word blasted out of her mouth. "It takes two to tango, baby."

"But—"

"Two!"

I sighed and closed my eyes, fighting the tears.

Molly was either psychic or she just knew me that well. "Aw, honey..."

"I'm fine," I said.

"You're not. But listen...either you have to deal with this or get out of the situation. Which is it going to be?"

"Get out?" I asked.

"Yeah. As in leave."

Frowning into my wine, I said, "I can't just leave. I have a contract." Well, I could leave. That ninety-day probationary period worked both ways.

"Is it the job...or him?"

"Both."

"And if it doesn't work out?" she asked softly.

I didn't have an answer.

Molly sighed. "So you have to decide. Either ride it out and hope for Prince Charming...and hey, maybe this is just a crush, right? You'll have some time to bank your money, maybe make some contacts and get some experience, right? Or you can quit and..."

I grunted. "Quit and do what? I think I'm stuck here, at least for a while."

"Look at it this way." Molly's voice took on a cheerful note. "You stuck it out with Emma *and* Gary for six months and made a lot less."

There wasn't a lot of humor in my laugh.

"Now...listen, you're feeling better already," Molly teased.

I tossed back half my wine and said, "No. Not really."

But yeah, actually I was. At least I had a plan of sorts.

Then I heard the door open and that plan seemed to evaporate. Dominic appeared in the doorway.

Shit.

Chapter 10

Aleena

"Molly, I have to go." I didn't wait for her to ask why or even for her to respond to my statement. I hung up the phone and set it aside, unable to look away from Dominic.

His face was pale and it dawned on me that he didn't look like he'd been sleeping well. He almost always had some five o'clock shadow going, even in the morning, but the scruff was thicker today.

In the weeks I'd known him, this was one of the few times I'd seen him look less than one hundred percent put together.

"Dominic." I stood.

"You're thinking about quitting," he said quietly.

I swallowed. Unable to meet his eyes, I turned away. "What are you talking about?" I asked quietly.

"I heard you."

The sound of his shoes on the marble floors had me tensing and I looked up to see his wavy reflection appear in the darkened windows just behind me. Pretending to busy myself with my food, I found the colander and drained my pasta. "Are you hungry? I always end up making more than..."

His hands came down on my shoulders.

"I heard you," he said again. "I guess you were talking to Molly. Are you leaving?"

With hands that shook, I put the colander down in the sink. Steam wafted from it as I slowly edged out from under his hands and faced him.

"No."

He caged me in up against the counter. Heat flooded me at the feel of his body against mine.

"Don't lie to me," he warned, his voice low. "I heard you talking about quitting."

"Yeah, *talking*." I jutted my chin up. "That doesn't mean I *am*. For now, I'm sort of stuck. So no. I'm *not* leaving."

His eyes flashed.

I tried to edge away and he brought up his arm, boxing me in. Before I could try the other side, he blocked that avenue as well. The air seemed a bit thicker than it had only a second ago.

"What..." I cleared my throat. "What are you doing?"

Instead of answering, he dipped his head and nuzzled my neck. "Do you know that the first time I saw you, I wanted you? When you fell against me that day in the restaurant, I had the insane idea...*I caught you. Can I keep you?*"

My breathing hitched.

"When we danced at the ball, I didn't want to let you go. When I had the chance to kiss you," he murmured. He paused and skimmed his lips down my throat. "I knew it was stupid, but I'd been waiting for that chance for too long. It felt like most of my life. I wasn't going to let it slip by."

He caught my earlobe and tugged on it lightly.

My knees tried to buckle then and he caught me up against him.

"You weren't supposed to do this, Aleena," he said, his voice going hard and flat. "You're in my head, in my thoughts, in my dreams."

I brought my hands up, bracing them on his chest between us.

"Being around you every day. Knowing you were so close and not being able to touch you," he said. "It made it so much worse."

"I need you," he whispered, his mouth just a breath from mine.

Half-afraid to move, I lifted my gaze to his.

His eyes blazed hot, so hot, I thought they might burn.

No, I was already burning and I wanted to beg him to touch me, to have me, to do whatever he wanted. But I couldn't give him what he needed.

I didn't know how.

"I think about you, too." The words escaped me before I could stop them.

He sucked in a breath and then, slowly, he lifted

his hands to cup my face. I took advantage of that and slipped away.

He spun on me and the glint in his eyes blazed hotter.

Refusing to give in to the need inside me, I shook my head. "But you don't need me, not really."

His eyes narrowed on my face.

"I work for you," I said, clearing my throat and going with the obvious and easiest route.

"We'll figure it out." Something passed across his features and was then gone behind that professional mask I hated. "Unless you don't want me."

My jaw dropped. Did he really think that? How could he think that? One touch from him and my entire body was singing. One look and my knees felt weak. I'd spent every minute of the past month denying how much I wanted him.

"I'm not what you want." I forced myself to say it. "I know that what we did the other night...it's not what you like."

A muscle in his jaw pulsed, but he said nothing.

Damn it. I was going to have to say it, wasn't I?

"The first weekend we were in the Hamptons, I went into the main house to explore." I looked down, unable to meet his eyes while I confessed. "I...um...heard you. And Maya. I wasn't sure what I was hearing, but I went upstairs...and..."

There was just the faintest sound and I jerked my head up.

"You saw," he said quietly.

Jerkily, I nodded my head.

"And?"

I stared at him. "What do you mean...and?" The blush staining my face so red was almost painful. Swallowing, I looked away.

Then he moved toward me.

It was just one small step, but I felt it.

His hand came up and cupped my cheek. I felt him tugging gently on my face, but I didn't want to look at him.

"What did you do, Aleena?"

The rough whisper was like a caress of silk down my spine. I shivered.

Then, as I was trying to figure out why I was suddenly, desperately turned on, he stroked his thumb across my lower lip, he leaned in and spoke softly into my ear. "What did you do, Aleena? You didn't run away screaming. Somebody would have heard. And you didn't quit, horrified by what you'd seen. So...what did you do?"

This time, when he tugged on my chin, I let him guide my face back to his.

"I watched," I said, the words coming out reluctantly.

"You watched." A slow smiled curled his lips. He leaned in closer and I almost moaned as he lifted an arm, bracing it on the island behind me—it was now a barrier just under my breasts, brushing up against me but not really touching me. "Did you like it,

Aleena? Did you like what you saw?"

I shivered.

"I'm going to kiss you now." He spoke with the same confidence he'd had when he'd kissed me that first time. "If you stop me, I'll respect your choice and it will never happen again."

I jerked my gaze up to his, watched as he shifted his weight until he was leaning lightly against me. "You...what?"

He traced my mouth with his thumb again.

"I'm going to kiss you. If you don't want me to, or if you don't want me, then stop me. We'll go back to business only. Or, if you prefer, we will terminate our relationship and you will be free to leave with the severance package outlined in your contract."

I'd pretty much stopped listening when he said he was going to kiss me.

He cupped my face and waited. When I didn't push him away or step back, he lowered his head. He started gentle, his lips soft as they pressed against mine. Then his lips parted and his tongue flicked against the corner of my mouth.

I opened with a sigh.

He made a sound and the kiss changed, became hungrier. Hardened. His teeth captured my bottom lip, worrying at it until I moaned. He sucked it into his mouth, soothing it with his tongue. It felt swollen as he released it, breaking the kiss and dropping his hands, but not moving away from me.

"I want you," he said, his voice calm. And his

eyes were...not. He stared at me with a hunger that was almost desperate. Then he slid a hand up and closed it around my neck. "I want you. You think you can't give me what I want? Then let me teach you, Aleena."

Well, damn.

Chapter 11

Aleena

Let me teach you...

"I want you, too." I could hardly believe I was saying the words. My stomach was on a crazy dance and my head wasn't much better. "But..."

He tensed, the grin on his face fading.

I hurried, wanting him to understand. "You need to know that when I said I wasn't experienced, I didn't just mean in the way you were doing things." My face was already so flushed that I didn't think I could blush any more deeply. "I've only been with one guy. I was fifteen and..."

I looked away.

Dominic slid the hand on my neck up into my hair. "Tell me," he murmured.

"It's a common enough story," I said, trying to smile. "Geeky girl, always acing the tests and messing things up for everybody else. Then a cute guy asked me to homecoming. He...um...he asked if I'd like to stop for a while on the way to the dance and I said yes."

Darting a look up at Dominic, I saw a muscle pulse in his jaw and jerked my gaze away again. "We...well, we had sex. It was my first time. I didn't really want to, but he talked about how much he liked me and, well, nobody ever had. So...I let him. It hurt."

I blew out a breath at the memory, knowing the most painful part is what happened next. "When we got to the dance, he told everybody." I remembered everything—the taunts, the pointed fingers, the girls whispering and laughing. One guy raising his hand and asking, "can I be next?"

"Want to know the worst part?" I said, a short bark bursting from my throat. "He hadn't wanted to take me at the dance. He just did it because one of his friends..." I stopped abruptly.

"Aleena."

Blowing out another breath, I made myself finish. "I'd been partnered with one of his football buddies as my lab partner. We were supposed to do a big project and the jock wasn't pulling his fair share. I told the dumb idiot that if he didn't do the work, that was fine, but he wouldn't get the credit. I finished the project and turned it in without his name on it. Short story is, the guy failed and couldn't play in four of the games that year. The dance, and what happened before, was payback. They all set it up, just to humiliate me."

An ugly snarl escaped him and his long body tensed. After a moment, he seemed to calm. His hands smoothed up and down my arms and he drew me up against him. "Did he hurt you?"

I shook my head. "He didn't force me." My voice was muffled against his chest. "He just didn't care that it was my first time. And..."

I stopped. I had sworn I'd never cry over that bastard again, but found the tears burning the back of my eyes. My throat clogged with the memory and a sob leaped from my mouth.

No!

Jerking away from him, I stormed over to where I'd left my wine and grabbed it, draining it in one long pull, trying to swallow the past with it. "The douche bag was an upper-class white boy." Holding out my arms as if displaying myself, I said, "Clearly, I am not white. He told me he'd heard that ghetto bitches like me were supposed to be nymphos, but I'd turned out to be a *real* disappointment."

My voice cracked.

Slamming the glass down, I turned away. "I've never even *been* to any kind frickin' ghetto," I said, sniffling. "There aren't even that many black people back home. One of my friends told me I was the whitest black person she ever knew."

I swiped at my tears as he came up behind me. Jerking my chin up, I glared at him. "I'm just a middle-class girl from a middle-class family and I'm *fine* with that. I'm biracial, but there's nothing ghetto about me." Then I cocked a brow at him. "If there *was*, I'd be just fine with it. But the son of a bitch only slept with me to hurt me and for revenge. Then, because I'm half-black, he thought that meant I'd be some kind of sex fiend who would enjoy the humiliation."

Dominic stroked a hand down my hair. "I'm sorry," he said quietly.

I sniffed once more. "Yeah, well." Recalling what Molly had told me, I said, "It is what it is, right?"

"And sometimes what it is sucks." He slid an arm around my waist. "Please tell me your next time was better, Aleena."

"Well...you tell me." I closed my eyes. "You were there."

He grew still and silent, I couldn't even hear him breathe. When he spoke, his voice was soft. "Please tell me that when we slept together, it wasn't only the second time you've ever had sex."

"Okay. I won't tell you."

"Shit." He turned me to face him. His fingers were gentle as he wiped away the lingering tears. "If I would've known, I would've..." He stopped and I watched him search for the words. "Hell, I can't say I would have been gentle. I wasn't in a good place." His thumb pressed against my lower lip. "Tell me I didn't hurt you."

"I enjoyed what we did," I said.

"That's not an answer," he countered.

104

"It was...intense." I chose my words carefully. "It may have hurt a bit, but not in a bad way. Not like before."

He moved closer and I backed up. I couldn't go far. The island was there and I found myself caged in, trapped between his body and the solid piece of kitchen furniture. "And when you saw me with Maya...was that intense? Did you enjoy watching me?"

"Yes," I whispered.

His face moved closer. "Do you want me to do any of that to you?"

"Yes."

"Do you want me to teach you?"

His mouth closed over mine. His tongue pushed inside my mouth, harder this time, driving inside with intent and purpose. I sucked on him and I felt his reaction in the way his body tensed against mine. I did it again and curled my arms around him, arching closer.

When he went to pull away, I did the same thing to him that he'd done to me several times—I bit his lower lip.

"You're going to test my self-control if you keep doing that," he said.

I scraped my teeth along his jawline before leaning back. "And then what would happen?"

He gave me a careful look. "I would need to show you who was in charge."

A thrill went through me as the danger of his

words collided with the promise in them. Gazing into his eyes, I considered him, knowing my world would change with just a few words. "I think I would like that."

His eyes turned the deep blue of a late night sky and his nostrils flared as he inhaled the breath I didn't realize he was holding. "Are you sure?"

I didn't know where the future was headed, or if we would regret this in the morning, but this moment in knew what I wanted. I nodded.

"If you want me to stop, just say red." He looked down at me.

"Why?" Blinking at him, I tried to process the sudden change in direction. "Why would I want you to stop?"

"It's called a safe word. Dominants use them with their subs in case they get too rough or go too far."

"How far..." My voice broke and something that might have been fear raced through me. "How far is too far? How rough is too rough?"

"Don't worry," he said, his voice gentle, almost soothing. "The control is in your hands. Just trust me. If you get nervous, if you're scared, just say the safe word and it all stops. And we'll start slow, baby. Now...what was the word?"

I licked my lips. "Red...?"

He tangled his hand in my hair and tugged, just as I'd seen him do with another woman.

"Exactly."

Oh fuck. This was really going to happen.

***

We ended up in the living room.

My food was going to get cold and I didn't care. It was the last thing on my mind. I was hungry for something else.

Dominic guided me into the wide, open area and backed up, leaving me alone in the middle of the floor.

"I want you to strip for me," he said, his voice the same tone I'd heard him use in board meetings and when talking to total strangers. But the eyes. His eyes were very different. He watched me with heat raging in his eyes. "Once you're naked, I'm going to spank you."

"Spank me?"

He pressed a finger to my mouth.

"Don't talk," he ordered.

"But..."

"You're being a bad girl, Aleena."

My breath shuddered out of me and I nodded.

"That's better." He shifted his hand to my neck, his thumb stroking along my jaw. "You said you were going to leave me." He bit down on my earlobe hard enough to make me gasp. "I'm going to punish you and then after..."

I swayed toward him. He steadied me.

"After," he said as he kissed the side of my neck. "After, I'm going to see how good you taste, then fuck you until you scream."

I liked that idea very much.

He stepped back, putting more distance between us this time. I started to ask what he was doing, but then he curled his fingers toward me. "Come take off my shirt."

I never would have thought that being given such an outright order would leave me so hot.

"Yes, sir," I whispered.

Then I froze. I'd spoken.

A faint smile curled his lips. "That's another punishment, Aleena."

We both heard the whimper that caught in my throat. Just as we both noticed the tremor in my fingers as I stripped his shirt away. I folded it and he took it away, dropped it carelessly on the nearest table before slanting a hot look at me.

"Now you. Strip."

There was no doubt that it was a command, and I hurried to obey. My shirt and pants went quickly enough and I had a moment to wish I'd worn something sexier than a matching set of plain white cotton undergarments.

"Bra first."

As I unhooked the front clasp and freed my breasts, I glanced at Dominic and my breath caught as I watched him stroke a hand up and down his cock through the fabric of his trousers. I let my eyes run down over his muscular chest and flat stomach. A thin line of golden hair ran from his bellybutton down to disappear inside the waistband of his trousers.

I went damp thinking about the feel of him inside me, his hands stroking over me.

"Your panties, Aleena. Now the panties."

I lowered them, feeling Dominic's eyes on me as I bent down before stepping out of them. As I straightened, I felt a flash of self-consciousness.

"Hands at your sides."

I hadn't even realized that I'd moved them to cover myself until he'd said it.

He circled me, moving closer with each pass until he was behind me. Through his trousers, I felt his cock rub against me. He reached around me and cupped my breasts.

"Exquisite." His breath was hot against my ear. "You have a beautiful body, Aleena. Never forget it. Never cover it."

His fingers closed around my nipples, rolling them as they hardened. I gave a startled yelp when he pinched them, but it was more from surprise than pain. The jolt that went through me was more pleasure.

"Hands on the arm of the couch."

I knew what was going to come after this and my stomach clenched. Part of it was nerves, but more was anticipatory desire. I moved towards the couch, feeling his eyes on me the entire way.

"You know what I'm going to do."

It was a statement more than a question, but I still nodded as I put my hands down. The position made me feel even more vulnerable than before. I flinched when his hand rested on my ass, but it was a caress. I closed my eyes, enjoying the sensation.

"Do you want this?"

I flushed.

My mind registered the crack a split second before the pain. It was a sharp sting that quickly faded to warmth, nothing more, but I still caught my breath.

"Answer me, Aleena. Do you want this?"

"Yes," I said, forcing the word out.

There was another slap, another sharp sting.

"You saw me doing this before, to another woman. Did you enjoy watching me?"

I whimpered.

"Answer me." His voice was firm. "Did it turn you on, watching me spank her?"

He spanked me when I didn't respond—twice. It took another hard smack before I could admit it. "Yes, sir!"

I couldn't believe I was admitting something so personal. Then again, I was bent over the couch getting spanked by my boss. It should've put things in perspective.

"How long did you stay?"

He didn't give me a chance to answer before his hand came down again, this time on the other cheek.

"I watched until you finished," I answered quickly, absorbing the pain of his last strike.

I felt more than saw him hesitate.

"You stayed from the time I spanked her until I came?"

"Yes."

I gasped as he spanked me again, twice in quick succession, one on either cheek and harder than before.

"What did you think?" he asked.

"I don't understand."

Two more smacks and my ass was burning now. The sting wasn't fading now, but was spreading through me, inching its way along my skin.

"When you saw me with her, what did you think?" He ran his hand up my back. "Did you think about what it must feel like, what I did to her? Did you wish you were her? Did you want to join us? Touch me? Touch her?"

The words popped out of my mouth before I could second-guess myself. "I thought you were beautiful."

The hand between my shoulder blades stopped and I hoped I hadn't said anything wrong.

"Stay there. Don't move." He sounded hoarse.

I forced myself to freeze, although, more than anything, I wanted to look at him. A minute passed. Then another. I dug my nails into the arm of the sofa, forcing myself not to turn. I thought he might have left. What was he—?

"Close your eyes," he said quietly. His voice was calmer now, a slow deep timber that vibrated through my spine.

Immediately, I closed them. Then I tensed as I felt him slipping something over my eyes.

"What are you—?"

"No talking, Aleena," he said as he finished fastening the blindfold into place.

I groaned and behind me, he laughed. Then he took my shoulders and guided me around. After weeks of living here, I had an idea of where he was going, just from where he moved me. He'd just nudged me over to the couch.

"Lie back," he said.

"What are we—?" I gasped as he brought his hand down on my ass, harder than before.

"I said *no talking.*"

Even as the pain flared in my bottom, he rubbed the area where he'd spanked me, soothing it. As he guided me to lie down, he started to speak. "Anything I do with you, I'll explain. But you have to show trust in me or this won't work...can you do that?"

I hesitated. Answer? Don't answer? I didn't know.

"You can answer when I ask you questions," he said and I felt him brush his lips across mine.

"Yes." I swallowed. "I can do that."

"Good." His hands skimmed down my breasts, caught my nipples and plucked them. I whimpered, but tried to strangle the sound.

"You don't need to do that. I want to hear what I do to you."

A sigh shuddered out of me.

"You're wearing the blindfold because I'm going to go down on you. Aleena, if I'm going to teach you how to play in my world, then you need to understand a few things. I'm a dominant. If you choose to be my submissive, you'll be the one kneeling in front of me. If I kneel in front of you, you won't see it happen." He slid a hand up my thigh. "If you can't handle that idea, then let me know."

I was still processing the '*I'm going down on you*' part of what he'd said.

"Aleena?"

I sucked in a breath and then said, "Uh...right now, it all sounds good to me."

He chuckled and I felt him kiss my knee.

Oh, *shit*.

"Open your legs."

Heat flooded my face and I slowly parted my thighs. I hissed as he pulled me towards the edge of the couch, the sensitive skin of my ass rubbing against the soft material.

With the blindfold on, everything seemed more intense. It didn't block out the light, but I was rendered blind nonetheless. His lips slid across my sex, while I was excruciatingly aware of the press of his fingers, even the feel of his knees pressing against my ankles as they dangled near the floor.

A shocked *"Oh..."* rolled out of me as he licked me.

He *licked* me, the same way he had licked my

mouth and my body exploded with sensation. Then he slid his tongue inside, teasing my entrance, going farther. Taunting me while I began to shudder and shake beneath him.

His teeth scraped over my clit and I cried out in startled, delirious pleasure.

I tugged and realized belatedly I'd curled my hands in his hair.

I went to pull them back, but he caught one, guiding it back to his scalp. "Don't stop," he muttered against me. "Show me that you want this."

Want it? I was trying to figure out how I'd ever existed *without* this.

He stiffened his tongue and pressed inside me again, starting to fuck me rhythmic thrusts. I flexed my hips, driving myself against his mouth, blindly seeking the orgasm I already felt building inside me.

I came hard and fast, and I forgot his order. I cried out his name and would have begged him not to stop, if I'd have the ability to think. But I'd long since lost that. I was still shuddering, shaking, sensation and hunger rolling through me when he pulled away.

I reached for him, but he caught my hands. "Be still," he said. His voice was tender, though, almost gentle.

My hands fell loose to my sides and I lay there, heart pounding. If I'd had the strength, I might have risked another punishment—although maybe it wasn't much of a risk since the...ah, consequences had been so pleasant. But I didn't have the strength.

"Come here," Dominic said, his voice low, quiet.

I would have asked, but his hands were on my hips, guiding me further off the edge of the couch. Those long, low cushions came in very handy.

I heard something tear, smelled something odd.

"A condom," he said softly.

"...do we...um, but you said you were clean..."

"I am." His fingers slid against me, distracting me as he continued to speak. "But I always wear one. Any woman I'm with should expect me to wear one—just as any woman should expect her partner to wear one."

I tried not to squirm at the idea of him so bluntly discussing his past lovers. "But..." I stammered. I didn't want a barrier between us. He'd felt so good the last time. "I won't get pregnant. And I've already told you that I've only been with the one guy. Why do we need one?"

"Because we do." His fingers slid inside me and pressed deep. I gasped as that simple touch sent sensation all but screaming through me.

"You're talking, Aleena," he murmured, bending low and nipping my lip. "This is one topic I'll excuse—this one time. But disobey me again and there will be punishment."

As if to highlight his words, he traced one hand down my hip and slid it under me, cupping my ass. It was both pleasure and pain and I already knew I wanted more.

"Are we clear?"

I nodded.

"Say the words."

"Yes, sir." The affirmation came quickly, without a moment's hesitation. I'd say anything, do anything to continue feeling this way.

Then his body brushed mine and the thought of obedience, punishment, pleasure, pain...everything, it all faded away and the only thing that mattered was him. This.

Instinctively, I reached up to push away the blindfold, but he caught my hands, held them in one hand and guided them overhead. "Not yet, Aleena," he whispered. "Not yet."

His cock pulsed against me as his mouth rubbed against mine, slowly, teasingly. When I tried to kiss him, he shifted his attention to my neck, my ear.

"Now, you're allowed to talk. I want to hear you beg. I want to hear you scream."

He bit my lower lip and I moaned.

"That will work, too."

I could almost hear the smile in his voice and then he kissed me and I tasted myself on his lips. It shouldn't have been so erotic. Yet I found myself rocking against him and sucking on his tongue, craving more.

He lifted his head and said, "You'll suck on my cock like that. Soon."

I lifted my mouth, seeking his.

"Won't you, Aleena?"

"Damn it, Dominic!"

"Answer the question." His voice was low, like a growl and his hand tightened around my wrists. "Will you suck my cock like that?"

"Yes...yes, sir." I shuddered as I said it, realizing now just how much I'd *longed* to do just that, to do just *this*...all of this.

"Good girl." He nipped my lower lip. "I'm tempted to sink into that sweet mouth right now, to feel those lips wrapping around me. Later. I want to feel that pussy of yours wrapped around me more."

"Yes, Dominic."

He passed over me, his sheathed cock slipping against my wetness. I whimpered when he rubbed against my clit.

"Now," he said after he'd done that so many times I started to shake.

He came inside me, driving in deep and hard. The skin on my bottom was sore and my clit felt swollen. *Everything* was more intense.

The hand restraining my wrists tightened and instinctively, I tugged against him.

"Remember how to make this stop," he said.

"I don't want you to stop."

"Good." He pressed his brow to mine, his breaths coming just as quickly as mine. And then he started to move.

He surged inside me, quick, deep thrusts that made me cry out. My back arched and I struggled to scream, struggled to breathe. Pleasure slammed into me, bombarded me.

And I begged.

"Please...please...please..." The word bounced and echoed off the walls and I thought if I didn't come soon, I'd die. Dominic moved higher on my body and the angle caused his cock to rub directly against my clit and I tensed, locking down around his cock.

It was too much—

"Scream for me."

I did.

I screamed until I couldn't breathe as the orgasm tore through me. Everything dimmed, grayed...and I felt his cock jerk and thicken as he started to come. He roared and continued to thrust, milking everything into me. Slowly, he quietened and slumped, his body coming down to rest on mine. I welcomed the weight and wrapped my legs around his waist, holding him tighter.

I whimpered.

Dazed, delighted...stunned.

Light blinded me and I blinked, realizing he'd taken the blindfold off. He pulled out and I gasped as that movement alone sent shockwaves of pleasure racing through me. He rose, left me—

I tensed, but he reappeared a moment later, carrying a blanket.

It was barely big enough for the two of us, but it didn't matter. He was big and warm and I'd never been so happy in my life.

But it came crashing to an ugly, grinding halt before the sweat even had a chance to dry on my skin.

The door unlocked and opened. I barely had a chance to sit up. Dominic's mother stood in the doorway, staring at us.

"Damn it, Dominic." She sighed.

Mortified, I clutched the blanket to my chest as Dominic shifted around to sit beside me.

"You know better than to sleep with the help."

The help?

A punch of humiliation slammed in me, so hard and fast I thought I'd be sick. Swallowing, I jerked a look at Dominic, but he just stared at his mother.

Jacqueline St. James-Snow sniffed and flicked me another look. "And really, Dominic, if you were in the mood for something...exotic, you could have found it elsewhere. Why bring it home?"

"Mom," Dominic said as his eyes hardened.

Slowly, I stood up.

I looked from Dominic to Jacqueline, wrapping the blanket more snugly around me. Before Dominic could say any more, I spoke, "I'm from Iowa, ma'am," I said, struggling to keep my voice level. "I really don't think you can consider a small-town girl like me *exotic*."

Then I grabbed my clothes, struggling not to let the tears fall as I hurried into the bathroom.

Exotic, she'd called me.

And Dominic had just *sat* there.

When I slid out of the bathroom a few minutes later, I darted a quick look his way. He rose and I scanned the room for my purse. I grabbed it along with my coat and hit the door before Dominic could stop me.

Never again, I vowed as I rode the elevator down to the lobby. I was through with him and the rest of this shitty city. He'd have to find someone else to serve him.

To be continued in Serving HIM Vol. 3, release June 1st

Acknowledgement

First, we would like to thank all of our readers. Without you, our books would not exist. We truly appreciate each and every one of you.

A big "thanks" goes out to all the Facebook fans, street team, beta readers, and advanced reviewers. You are a HUGE part of the success of the series.

We have to thank our PA, Shannon Hunt. Without you our lives would be a complete and utter mess. Also a big thank you goes out to our editor Lynette and our wonderful cover designer, Sinisa. You make our ideas and writing look so good.

About The Authors

M. S. Parker is a USA Today Bestselling author and the author of the Erotic Romance series, Club Privè and Chasing Perfection.

Living in Southern California, she enjoys sitting by the pool with her laptop writing on her next spicy romance.

Growing up all she wanted to be was a dancer, actor or author. So far only the latter has come true but M. S. Parker hasn't retired her dancing shoes just yet. She is still waiting for the call for her to appear on Dancing With The Stars.

When M. S. isn't writing, she can usually be found reading– oops, scratch that! She is always writing.

2. Cassie Wild

Cassie Wild loves romance. Every since she was eight years old she's been reading every romance novel she could get her hands on, always dreaming of writing her own romance novels.

When MS Parker approached her about co-authoring the Serving HIM series, it didn't take Cassie many seconds to say a big yes!!

Serving HIM is only the beginning to the collaboration between MS Parker and Cassie Wild. Another series is already in the planning stages.

Made in the USA
Las Vegas, NV
06 October 2021